The Menfolk Are Missing!

It had been more than a month and a half since he had left Fort Hall when he crested a grassy ridge and saw a lone wagon traveling across the valley below. A wagon with no men around that he could see. And, despite his determination to continue his quest, his good side rose up and forced him to go see just what had brought these women out here with a wagon and no menfolk. He was pretty certain it would not be a good story.

A couple of hours later, he was sitting at a fire with three women—one young, not yet out of her teens, and very pretty; one who was obviously the young woman's mother, in her thirties, perhaps, and not unattractive; and an older woman who still looked good—waiting for them to tell their tale . . . .

Don't miss the first book in the series . . .

WILDGUN

Wildgun
Vengeance Trail

Jack Hanson

JOVE BOOKS, NEW YORK

This is a work of fiction. Names, characters, places, and incidents are either the product of the author's imagination or are used fictitiously, and any resemblance to actual persons, living or dead, business establishments, events or locales is entirely coincidental.

VENGEANCE TRAIL

A Jove Book / published by arrangement with the author

PRINTING HISTORY
Jove edition / January 2000

The Penguin Putnam Inc. World Wide Web site address is http://www.penguinputnam.com

ISBN: 0-515-12732-9

A JOVE BOOK®
Jove Books are published by The Berkley Publishing Group, a division of Penguin Putnam Inc., 375 Hudson Street, New York, New York 10014.
JOVE and the "J" design are trademarks belonging to Penguin Putnam Inc.

PRINTED IN THE UNITED STATES OF AMERICA

10 9 8 7 6 5 4 3 2 1

Wildgun
Vengeance Trail

Prologue

WILL BARLOW SPOTTED the lonely wagon creaking slowly across the small valley floor when he topped a grassy ridge. He pulled his big mule, Beelzebub, to a halt and watched for a few moments. He wanted to make sure it was out of sight before he rode down there. He was looking for his daughter, Anna, and did not want to waste time jawing with some pilgrims.

But as he watched the ox-drawn wagon, something about it bothered him. Then it came to him—there were no men to be seen, just three women and several children. It was definitely odd. Barlow sighed. He could not let a wagon of nothing but women and children journey on alone. At the least, he had to find out what had brought them here.

"C'mon, Buffler," he said to the huge black Newfoundland dog who stood alongside the mule, "let's go see what the doins' are with those folks." He walked the mule slowly down the slope of the rise, each step jolting his backbone. His two pack mules protested mildly. Once on the flat, however, he picked up the pace and swiftly closed the gap with the sluggish rolling wagon. As he neared the noisy Conestoga, he shouted a greeting, wanting the women to know he was approaching in a friendly manner.

Still, one of the women turned to face him and lifted her rifle. He hoped she would wait before firing. She did, and she lowered the weapon when Barlow pulled to a stop a few feet from her. She remained wary, however.

"My name's Will Barlow, ma'am," he said quietly. "There any menfolk around?"

When the woman hesitated, Barlow said, "I ain't seen any. They off huntin', or did you have some hard doing's?"

The woman still said nothing; she just stood there looking flustered and worried. She was in her late forties, Barlow figured, and probably had been beautiful as a girl. She was still somewhat attractive, though a hard life had left its mark on her. She was fairly tall, and while not exactly willowy, was certainly not stout. Though life had taken its toll, she retained enough shapeliness and inner spirit to hold more than a little appeal. Her dress was tattered and worn. Dirt and worry covered her face, but there was no real fear in her deep green eyes.

"Somethin' happen to your menfolk?" Barlow asked. He wanted to look around to see if the men weren't hiding somewhere nearby for some reason. But this woman's nervousness, and her holding the rifle kept his attention riveted to her.

"Um . . . Well, we . . . they . . ."

Barlow leaned forward a little and patted Beelzebub's big neck. "Look, ma'am, I ain't here to do you no harm. If you're facin' hard doin's here, might be I could help you."

Another woman suddenly spoke up: "Tell him, Gran."

Barlow turned his head to look at her. She was a much younger version of the one with the rifle, and showed what the armed woman must have looked like thirty years or so ago. She was perhaps seventeen, with golden hair that hung well past her shoulders. Soil and tiredness could not disguise the beauty of her face nor the fire in her greenish eyes. Barlow turned his attention back to "Gran."

The woman's shoulders sagged, but then she squared them and nodded. "What was your name again, Mister?"

"Will Barlow."

"I'm Hope Skinner, Mr. Barlow. Light and tie. It's getting' nigh onto dark, and we might's well call it a night here."

"Seems to be a more likely spot right over yonder," Barlow said, pointing to a small copse of cottonwoods and willows a few hundred yards away.

Hope nodded, and turned. In a moment, she had issued some orders, and the wagon and its small entourage were moving. Two children marched along, one more rode on a little seat on the side of the wagon, the youngest woman continued to carry the child at her hip, and the two women—plus a third one of an age between the two others, who had appeared from behind the Conestoga—guided the vehicle along.

As they rode, Barlow asked, "How're you folks fixed for meat?"

"None fresh," Hope replied. "Got some salted beef left, if you're of a mind."

"I'll be back directly," Barlow said. "There's still time for this ol' chil' to make meat."

When he returned, half an hour or so later, the women had the oxen unhitched and hobbled where they could feed on the grass, and had a fire going with a large pot of coffee setting on a rock almost in the flames, and a store of firewood set by. Barlow nodded, pleased but not really surprised at the women's efficiency. He dismounted and carted the antelope carcass to the fire, where he squatted and began skinning it. Buffalo curled up beside him.

"You want me to tend to your horse, Mister?" a boy of about eleven asked. He was the oldest child Barlow had seen here.

"What's your name, son?" Barlow asked.

"Charley."

Barlow nodded. "Well, Charley, ol' Beelzebub there is a mule," he said evenly. "But I'd be mighty obliged was you to see to him."

The boy nodded and ran off, proud and happy. As he did, a girl of about eight shyly wandered up. "My name's Rachel," she announced quietly. "Will your doggie hurt me, Mister?" she asked.

Barlow smiled, though a twinge of pain lanced his heart. He thought that maybe little Anna would look a little like this shy young girl in a few years. If he could ever get her back from the damned Indians who had her. He forced himself to abandon that thought for the time being. "You fixin' to hurt him?" he asked, regaining his smile.

"Oh, no, I'd never do nothin' like that," the girl, wide-eyed with wonder.

"Then you go right on and pet him, chil'," Barlow said quietly. "His name's Buffler, and he likes to have his ears scratched right where they come up out of his head. And, Buffler, you be on your best behavior with this lass."

The midnight-dark dog raised its great furry head and almost seemed to grin at his master. He quietly accepted the tentative petting from the little girl.

Not long after, they were eating roasted antelope and sipping hot coffee. "So," Barlow asked, "how'd you ladies and your young'ns come to be out here by yourselves?"

1

WILL BARLOW THOUGHT, as he did every time he saw one of the villages of Indians out here in the Oregon country, that it was a mighty dilapidated place. The Umpquas were a drab, shabby-looking lot compared with the Nez Percé and the other tribes back in the Rocky Mountains or out on the Plains. But he had no sympathy or warmth in his heart for the poor Umpquas. They were the ones who had attacked his small spread last fall, killed his wife, Sarah, and son, Little Will, and stolen his daughter, Anna. And, after a winter spent torn between rage and self-pity, Barlow was bent on getting Anna back.

"How long're we gonna wait here, hoss?" Dan Richwine asked.

Barlow glanced at the man. He was one of five men with Barlow on this raid into Umpqua country. Barlow had found Richwine and the four others at Fort Vancouver during the spring when he had wandered into the Hudson's Bay Company post on the northern shore of the mighty Columbia River. As they were all Americans—something still mighty unusual in these parts, Barlow had bought them all a few rounds of whiskey.

In the doing, he had explained his plight—and his plans. The five Americans, not feeling any pain from the liquor, had decided to throw in with Barlow.

"Not much longer, Barlow said. "It's gettin' close to dark, and someone ought to come wanderin' up this way soon."

"Hell, why don't we just go in and grab someone?" Bob Carruthers asked. He was a tall, thick-waisted, thick-headed man whom Barlow didn't trust one iota.

"That'd raise a ruckus," Barlow explained.

Carruthers shrugged. "Ain't no trouble with that, far's I can see."

Barlow shook his head in annoyance. He regretted now having asked these men to come along. He didn't care for any of them, though Floyd Balinger was a halfway decent fellow. The others—Richwine, Carruthers, Eli Whitfield and Mark Aikens—were a thoroughly disreputable bunch: mean, vicious, without charity. While Barlow hated the Umpquas, he could not bring himself to hate all Indians for the troubles brought on by a few. Not when his wife had been half Chinook. But these others, they seemed to think nothing of wanting to kill Indians for whatever reason, or for no reason.

On the other hand, Barlow felt more comfortable traveling through this country with company. And the others would come in handy when it came time to raid the right village and rescue his daughter. They could butcher all the Umpquas they wanted then, he figured, while he grabbed Anna and got her out of there. He had no love for the Umpquas, and would not be saddened if numbers of them died at the hands of his companions. Not if it would help him get Anna back.

"Here comes some ol' hoss," Whitfield said. His reedy, scratchy voice sounded almost eager. He was a wizened man, with long white hair and a matching beard and mustache. He had been around forever, it appeared, and he had lost whatever compassion for his fellow man that he might have once possessed.

"Eli, you and Mark go take him," Barlow ordered

softly. "Jist remember to bring him back here alive and not too hurt."

"What the hell do you care if he's hurt some?" Richwine asked.

"Don't," Barlow whispered. "But if this ain't the right village, I aim to let him go—if he can tell me where Anna is. I got no love for any of these Umpquas, but I don't need a passel of 'em followin' us, half froze to raise our hair."

Aikens and Whitfield returned minutes later, towing an unfortunate Umpqua. The warrior appeared to be scared half to death, but Barlow suspected at least some of that was an act. An old piece of cloth was tied around his mouth.

"Let's go," Barlow said, rising and stalking off through the dripping trees. He was plumb sick of all the rain and wetness in this land. They tossed the Umpqua over a pack mule and tied him down. Then they mounted their animals, and rode out. They had made a camp for themselves two miles from here, when they had first spotted the village.

At the camp, the warrior was tied to a tree, while the six Americans poured themselves coffee. Finally Barlow approached the Indian and untied the gag. He squatted in front of the captive, and asked in poorly pronounced Umpqua, "Where's the white girl who was taken last fall?"

"I don't know," the Umpqua said flatly.

"I'll hurt you bad if you don't tell me what I want to know," Barlow said. His voice was calm, reasoned, but there was no mistaking the steel underlying the words.

"I don't know," the Umpqua repeated, face set in determination.

"Not only will I hurt you, boy, but I'll hurt your whole goddamn village if I go riding in there looking for my daughter," Barlow said, reverting to English.

The Umpqua looked into Barlow's eyes, and he did not like what he saw there. He had heard about this white-eyed devil, the one who with only one companion had driven off a war party of Umpquas, killing a few. This man, the Umpqua knew, was dangerous, and if he could read people correctly, he knew that Barlow would do just what he said he would.

"She belongs to Red Cedar," the warrior said. "His village is half a day walk northwest of here. Along Cow Creek."

Barlow nodded. "You know that I'll be back and cut your heart out if I learn you've lied to me, don't you?"

The Umpqua nodded.

Barlow considered leaving right away, but decided that would be foolish. It was well into the afternoon, and they would not get far before night overtook them. He had waited this long, he could wait a little longer, though he was not entirely comfortable with the thought.

Barlow awoke in the morning to find the Umpqua dead, still tied to the tree. That angered him, but there was nothing that could be done about it. "What happened to him?" he asked as he filled a tin mug with coffee.

"He was snorin' somethin' awful," Bob Carruthers said with a derisive chuckle. "Disturbin' my slumbers. So I put him out of my misery." He broke into laughter, and was joined by everyone but Barlow.

Barlow waited until the laughter died down, then said, "Well, looks like you had your little bit of fun. But if any of you fractious bastards crosses me again, I'll carve your heart out and feed it to Buffler here."

The others looked warily at him. Even Carruthers, who was a big, powerful man, would think twice before voluntarily tangling with Will Barlow, who was not very tall, but he was built like a chunk of mountain. While only about 5-foot-9, Barlow packed almost two hundred fifty pounds on his frame. He had a bull neck, huge thighs, and big, powerful arms. His face was broad, and dominated by a nose that was rather flattened from being broken several times in various fights. All that, combined with his shock of long, unkempt, straw-colored hair and dark, expressive eyes gave the others pause.

No one argued with him, and breakfast passed quickly and quietly. Soon they were loading the pack animals and saddling their riding mounts. As another rain shower started, they clomped slowly out of camp, Barlow in the lead, the others strung out single file behind him.

Though the misty cloudiness would not allow the six hard men to see the smoke of the Umpqua village fires, they could smell it from a quarter-mile away. They stopped and dismounted, tying their horses and mules to tall pines.

"What now, ol' hoss?" Richwine asked as they all stretched. It was midafternoon, but with the omnipresent grayness there was little heat, though it was June.

"Find us a talkative critter from yon village," Barlow said.

"Ye aim to set here and wait all damn day like we done yesterday?" Carruthers asked. He was an impatient man at the best of times.

"If need be." As was usual with Barlow, his eyes were taking in everything around him, constantly searching, wary. "But it don't appear that'll be necessary." He pointed.

His five companions turned. A short line of Umpqua warriors was weaving through the dense trees. The men appeared to be toting a couple of deer carcasses.

"Let's go," Barlow said harshly. "Jist remember, boys, I want one of them critters alive. And do it quiet. I don't want that whole goddamn village out to raise our hair."

They melted into the trees; silent, deadly shadows in the deeper shadows of the wet pine forest. They were used to moving with stealth, though it wasn't entirely necessary now, as the Umpquas were talking among themselves as they headed toward their nearby village. They had no reason to fear anyone.

Led by Barlow, the small group of former mountain men suddenly rushed forward, tomahawks or knives in hand. Barlow went straight for an Umpqua hunter near

the front of the line of men. He slammed into the Umpqua, his shoulder hitting hard against the Indian's elk-
skin armor. It rocked the Umpqua, and he went down,
his fur cap sailing off into the underbrush. Barlow
pounced on top of him, grabbing him by the throat and
squeezing. He held on until the Umpqua started to lose
consciousness. He released the man and stood. "Watch
him, Buffler," he told his big dog. Then he turned and
headed into the fray again.

The Newfoundland growled at the Umpqua, though
the warrior would not present a threat anytime soon.

Barlow's help really wasn't needed, however. His
companions had been savage, and the attack on the
small hunting party had swiftly turned into a massacre.
The Umpquas were not prepared for the surprise raid;
the white men were hell-bent on killing, and all of the
Umpquas but the one were dead before they could rally
any kind of defense.

Barlow said nothing when his companions scalped the
Umpquas they had killed. But when the short, gruesome
task was done, he said to Richwine, "Dan, bring along
that ol' hoss I caught." Without waiting for an answer,
he called, "C'mon, Buffler, let's go." He stalked back to
their animals. The others quickly joined him.

There had been little sound during the entire melee,
and the white men were still quiet as they gathered by
their animals. Their captive was afraid and worried in
the harsh grip of the mean-faced Dan Richwine.

"Toss that critter up on one of the mules," Barlow
ordered.

"We goin' somewhar?" Mark Aikens asked. He didn't
much care one way or the other, he just wanted to know.

Barlow nodded. "We'll go make us a camp somewhere a bit away from here," he said. "Where we can
parley with this ol' red devil."

The others shrugged and mounted their animals after
tying the Umpqua to one of the mules. Whitfield and
Floyd Balinger rode swiftly to where the "battle" had
taken place and gathered up the two deer the hunters

had been toting back to their village. "Might's well make use of fresh meat," Whitfield said, proud of his practicality, as he and Balinger rejoined the group.

A little more than an hour later, Barlow stopped in a small clearing and looked around. Then he nodded. "This'll suit," he said as he dismounted.

The others did so, too. Soon after the captive was tied to a tree, the animals had been unloaded or unsaddled and tended to, the sparse stores of supplies were stacked and covered, firewood had been gathered, a fire started, the deer skinned and butchered, meat was cooking and coffee heating.

The men took their time, eating a leisurely meal and then puffing on pipes while relaxing with coffee. It was just about dark now, the ever-present cloudiness aiding in the early nightfall.

Finally Carruthers asked, "You about ready to start jawin' with that Umpqua, Will?" He sounded eager to get to it.

Barlow thought that over for a minute, his face clouded by smoke from his small clay pipe. "Reckon it'll hold till mornin'," he finally said. "Let that hoss fret a while, wonderin' what we aim to do with him."

The others grumbled, but could see some wisdom in it. Most soon after headed for their sleeping robes or blankets. Barlow sat up for a while, eyes glaring at the unknowing Umpqua. His hate for the warrior—and all Umpquas—was almost palpable. He wanted nothing more than to go over there and start peeling the skin from the Indian, one small strip at a time. But while that would perhaps give him some satisfaction by exacting some form of revenge, it would do nothing to help him get Anna back, and that was the most important thing. So he just sat there, watching the Umpqua with hooded eyes and letting his hate fester. He might need that deep-down hate to do what was necessary to make the Umpqua talk.

Finally, however, he stretched out in the otter sleeping robe that Sarah had made for him shortly before they

had married. It was warm and waterproof. And it kept
her memory close to him. And on this night, memories
of her were strong. They flooded his mind as he tried to
fall asleep. He could see her in all sorts of ways, as if
she were right there—working around their small cabin,
or out in the little garden she insisted on having in addition to their other planting. He could see her tending
to the children, breast-feeding Little Will, smiling as she
crooned either a Scottish lullaby or some Chinook tune.

But mostly, at times like this, when he was missing
her desperately, he could see her in their bed. Underneath him, her face lightly coated with the sweat of lust;
or atop him, her heavy, womanly breasts bouncing
wildly in the throes of her passion. He could almost feel
her breasts in his hands, and the way he felt almost
afraid to touch them—they were so soft and smooth, and
he worried that the calluses on his life-hardened hands
would feel too rough. But she never objected; indeed,
she had usually taken his hands and guided them to her
bosom, and her rapidly rising, hardening nipples let him
know it was the right thing. She was a picture of beauty
and womanliness to him, her dark skin and red-tinged
hair powerfully attractive to him. Her love, warmth and
caring were mighty powerful inducements to loving her.

He growled at himself and tried to force himself to
sleep, but it was a while in coming.

2

THE AMERICANS AWOKE within minutes of each other, and rapidly broke their fast with more deer meat and coffee. After a relaxing pipe, Barlow pushed himself up and headed toward the Umpqua. He was only a little reluctant about what he was going to do. He was not a cruel man by nature, and did not like the thought of possibly having to torture this man. On the other hand, his hate was powerful, and his quest honorable, and that made the prospective job a little less onerous. The knowledge that it would—hopefully—put Anna back into his arms again helped steel his mind.

He squatted in front of the Indian. "You speak English, boy?" he asked evenly.

The Umpqua nodded once, tentatively.

"Good. What's your name?"

"Gray Hawk."

"All right, Gray Hawk, some Umpquas raided my place last fall. Kilt my wife and son and stole my daughter. Somebody in your village has her. I want to know who, and I want to know how she's doin'."

"No white girl here," the Umpqua said.

Barlow smashed Gray Hawk in the face with a massive, hard-knuckled fist, cracking the orbital bone around the Umpqua's left eye. The Indian grunted.

"Now, I know you're lyin'," Barlow said. "And I'm not of a mood to be kind. I want my daughter back, and you'll help me, or by God, I'll carve you to pieces."

"Not lying. White girl not here!"

The Umpqua was afraid. Barlow could easily see that, but something else about the man's look or voice gave him momentary pause. "Was she here?"

"Yes," Gray Hawk said with a sharp nod. "Was here. Gone now."

"Where is she?"

"Not sure." Gray Hawk winced as he awaited another punch from Barlow.

But the American instead said, "Tell me what you know."

"Red Cedar, a war chief, brought her here. He kept her." Gray Hawk licked his lips. "Coffee?" he asked.

"When you tell me what I want to know."

Gray Hawk nodded. "Red Cedar lose girl in hand game."

"He lost her wagerin' on a goddamn game of hand?" Barlow snapped, rage bursting into full bloom inside him. He managed to control himself after a bit.

"Yes."

"Shit." Barlow swore in irritation. "To who?" he asked harshly.

"Some Shoshonis. A band visited two moons ago. They had come from their land far to the east to trade."

Barlow squatted there for some minutes, pondering what he had learned. He had hoped beyond hope that he would have Anna back by this evening, but now that was out of the question—if Gray Hawk was telling the truth. He pushed himself up. "One of you boys give this critter some coffee, and a bit of meat," he said.

"What fer?" Richwine countered. "We're jist gonna make wolf bait out of his red hide."

"Not jist yet we ain't," Barlow snapped.

"But you got the information you needed," Richwine responded.

"Suppose he ain't tellin' us the truth?" Barlow said harshly. "No, we wait till I check out that village. Now feed him and let him be."

Once more, Barlow squatted in front of Gray Hawk. It was late afternoon, and the slate sky was already beginning to darken into night. "Where is Red Cedar's place in the village?" he asked.

Gray Hawk's face was contorted from the severe pain of his cracked face. The cheekbone was swollen and discolored. His eyes were glassy, and he shook his head slowly in response to the question.

"Tell me, Gray Hawk," Barlow insisted. "Or we'll go in there and jist start raisin' hair on your people till I find out."

"Water first," Gray Hawk said quietly.

"Bring me some water over here," Barlow ordered. He waited until someone handed him a wooden canteen, which he uncorked and held up so that the Umpqua could take a drink.

When Gray Hawk had had his fill, he closed his eyes for a moment against the pain in his face. Then he said, "Red Cedar has the biggest lodge. Made of cedar planks. No bark. It's toward northwest."

Barlow nodded. He pulled his knife and reached slowly out. Gray Hawk's eyes widened a moment despite his pain, but Barlow only cut the rawhide thongs holding the elkhide armor over his buckskin shirt. Barlow pulled the armor—which could easily turn an arrow—loose, though not without some struggle, and stood. He hung it over his stout frame, and then pulled a couple of whangs from the sides of his buckskin pants and used them to tie the armor on. He needed the extra length the rawhide fringes gave him, since he was so much broader in the chest and shoulders than Gray Hawk was.

"What the hell you need that damn thing fer?" Eli Whitfield asked.

"It'll help throw off my scent with the dogs over in the village," Barlow said flatly. He grimaced at Buffalo when the Newfoundland sniffed warily at him. "It's me, dammit, and you damn well know it," Barlow growled.

Barlow climbed onto his mule, and watched as the others mounted their animals. "When we git there," he said, "I aim to go in alone. We sure as hell don't need the lot of us stumblin' around that village. I want you boys to keep your quiet, but be ready in case them critters catch on that I'm there and start a ruckus. If that happens, you boys're free to stir up as much hell as you want. Jist make sure you don't raise hair on me by mistake."

They rode out, leaving Gray Hawk tied to the tree, in pain and chanting something that Barlow assumed was a death song of some sort. As he rode along, Barlow let his anger build. He was furious, not only at having missed a chance to recover his daughter, but also that Red Cedar had so callously lost Anna by gambling. The thought of some Umpqua putting Anna up as a wager on a silly game knotted his stomach and filled him with rage. And Barlow was determined to make Red Cedar pay for his many atrocities.

The group stopped less than a hundred yards from the perimeter of the village, which consisted of cabins made of cedar planks or bark. The men could see little of the village but its outline because it was full dark, and with the usual complement of clouds, there was virtually no moonlight or starlight.

"Stay here, Buffler," Barlow said. Without another word he slipped off into the darkness, a wraith with revenge in his heart. He edged silently into the village, where some of the mongrels gathered in confusion around him, sniffing suspiciously. Barlow growled low in his throat and half jumped at the dogs. They backed off, whimpering and growling, but they left him alone after that.

Barlow stole through the sleeping Umpqua village, sizing up cabins as he did. When he was sure he had found the largest one, he stopped at the open entrance and waited, listening. Hearing nothing out of the normal, he slid inside, where it would have been even darker were it not for the glowing embers of the fire. He waited a few more moments, letting his eyes adjust as much as possible.

Something moved along one wall, and it soon resolved itself into the shadow of a man just beginning to mount a woman from behind. The woman moaned.

Barlow grinned grimly and moved toward the coupling couple. He was as silent and as determined as death. He suddenly grabbed a handful of the Umpqua man's hair, jerked his head back and placed a knife to his Adam's apple. Before the Umpquas could really react, he said in their language, "Either of you makes a sound, and I'll cut your throat.

The man grunted acknowledgement.

Barlow slipped a rawhide loop around the man's neck and stood, pulling the noose tight. "She makes any ruckus," he said in English, "you'll die, and then I'll come back for her. You understand that, Red Cedar?"

"You know my name?" the Umpqua countered, surprised.

"Yep. You understand?"

"Yes."

"Good. Now, woman, tie his hands behind him."

Frightened, the woman did so. She was still naked, and her body glowed a warm dark pink in the ember light. She wasn't half bad looking, Barlow noted. Under other circumstances, he might have been interested in her.

The woman finished, and Barlow nodded. "Remember what I said, woman," he said harshly. "Let's go, Red Cedar." Barlow wrapped the end of the rawhide rope around his hand until his fist was only about a foot from Red Cedar's neck. They walked swiftly across the village and into the woods where Barlow's companions waited.

Two hours later, the group was back in the white men's camp, where Red Cedar was tied, standing, to a tree a few feet from a pain-racked Gray Hawk, who was still sitting.

"You two boys have a nice talk," Barlow said. "Me and my friends're gonna catch us some robe time. We'll parley with you in the mornin'."

Gray Hawk must have talked to Red Cedar considerably during the night, because the war leader watched with fear-flecked eyes as Barlow approached him in the morning. "Why you hate me?" Red Cedar asked when Barlow stopped in front of him. "Why you want to do this to me? I your friend."

Barlow snapped out a fist, breaking Red Cedar's nose. "You ain't no friend of mine, you skunk-faced son of a bitch," Barlow snarled. "You stole my daughter, you festerin' heap of clam shit, and then you lost her on a wager. Jesus goddamn Christ, you are one sad son of a bitch."

"Not know what you mean," Red Cedar offered.

Barlow's fist made a mush of the Umpqua's face. And then he ground a thumb into Red Cedar's left eye. "You are a villainous critter with a heart black as a bear's asshole," he said vehemently. "I want to know who won my girl from you in that hand game."

"Not know what you mean," Red Cedar repeated.

"You ain't only a nasty bastard, but you're as dumb as dirt," Barlow said. His rage had reached a high boil, and sustained him in what he was about to do—what he felt he had to do. He pulled his Green River knife, the one he used for butchering, with the slightly curved blade. Then he began slicing a line down Red Cedar's chest, a little to the left of the sternum. It was barely deep enough to draw a thin line of blood.

Red Cedar hissed once with the sudden pain, but then clamped his mangled lips together.

Barlow slit a parallel line about the same distance to the right of the Umpqua's breastbone. Then he connected the two slits with one across the top. With the tip of the blade, Barlow worked the skin free from the muscle underneath until he had enough to grasp with his fingers. He suddenly yanked, tearing the skin down and away, until the strip of bloody flesh dangled down below Red Cedar's waist.

Barlow tore several more strips of skin from the Indian's chest, pulling each one loose more slowly than the last, until Red Cedar had almost a skirt of his bloody chest and stomach skin fluttering in the breeze around his midsection.

Barlow looked into the Umpqua's pain-racked eyes and smiled grimly. "Who was the critter you gave my daughter over to?" he asked in an icy voice.

Red Cedar shook his head.

Seething, Barlow turned and walked to the fire, as his five companions watched in puzzlement. He poured himself a mug of coffee and had a sip before walking back to stand in front of the Indian. He slowly took another sip, his eyes burning into Red Cedar's. Then he suddenly jerked the cup forward, and the steaming liquid splashed across Red Cedar's raw, quivering flesh.

Red Cedar groaned and sagged against the ropes that held him up. "No talk," he gasped.

Gray Hawk muttered some phrases in Umpqua. Barlow understood enough to know that he was telling Red Cedar to tell the white man what he wanted to know. But Red Cedar had gotten a determined look in his eyes, despite the agony.

Dan Richwine began walking toward the men's small store of supplies, saying over his shoulder, "I got something that might loosen that red devil's tongue fer him." He returned in a moment with the group's little sack of salt, stopping next to Barlow. He grinned a vicious grin. "Let's jist see how ye like these doin's, you fish-eatin' son of a bitch," he said, almost cheerily, as if he were enjoying himself. He opened the bag and poured a tiny mound of salt crystals onto his palm. With the suddenness of a striking snake, he slapped the palm against Red Cedar's bloody, skinned chest, and ground the salt into the raw flesh.

Red Cedar gasped and his chest tried to shrink away from the sizzling pain, but there was nowhere for it to go. His eyes rolled up into his head and he started to droop, on the verge of unconsciousness.

"Oh, no ye don't, boy," Richwine said. He grabbed the Umpqua's left earlobe and pinched it hard. That snapped the warrior back to some semblance of alertness. "Now, my amigo here asked ye a question. I think ye'd best answer it or ye'll feel pain like ye nary imagined." Richwine began pouring salt into his hand agin.

"I talk," Red Cedar moaned. "I talk."

"Who was it you dealt my daughter to, goddammit?" Barlow demanded.

"Shoshonis," Red Cedar gasped.

"Who amongst them varmints?" Barlow asked, voice raspy with hate. "What's the bastard's name?"

"White Bear," the Umpqua said,

Barlow nodded. He would be able to find Anna now. It would not be easy, but it could be done. And there was nothing more this Umpqua could tell him that would help get him any closer. "It's a good thing you finally spoke up, you reprobate," he said. "Now your death will be a mostly easy one." He turned and walked toward his saddle. "Let's go, boys," he said. "We got some ridin' ahead of us."

"You gonna jist leave them two critters there like that?" Mark Aikens asked. He was not the brightest of fellows.

"Yep," Barlow threw over his shoulder, not slowing.

"But ain't we gonna make 'em suffer some more for what they done before we kill 'em?"

Bob Carruthers suddenly laughed. "They'll be gittin' their payback right fine, boy," he said, still laughing. "There's wolves and coyotes and bears and other critters gonna find them two bastards right tasty, 'specially that there one with his chest meat all out to the open like it is. And them two have to jist stand there waitin' for it to happen."

Barlow said nothing, just started saddling Beelzebub, but he felt deep inside that this was fair payment for what Red Cedar had done to Anna.

3

NOW THAT HE had a new idea of where Anna might be, Barlow burned with a desire to head out after her. But he had to use his head or he would not have much of a chance of finding his daughter. So he forced himself to wait while the others saddled their horses, and they all loaded supplies. Then they rode off, heading north. As they traveled, Barlow decided that the smartest thing would be to get to Fort Vancouver and pick up some supplies. There was no telling how long it would take him to run down the right band of Shoshonis in all the country over which the tribe held sway. And to head out there with no supplies would be suicidal.

Fort Umpqua was fairly close, but it was a small, pitifully maintained place and would be unlikely to have enough extra supplies for six men planning a long mission. Then there was the fact that between the six of them, they couldn't afford enough supplies to get them fifty miles. At Fort Vancouver, Barlow was certain he could talk his father-in-law or even the factor, Dr. John McLoughlin, into loaning or giving him the supplies. His father-in-law, Duncan Stewart, would be certain to do so, if it meant the possible recovery of his grand-daughter.

So he pressed on hard, barely talking to his five companions, who grumbled considerably at the pace Barlow set. But Barlow did not care what they thought. All of his energies were focused on making Fort Vancouver and then heading eastward as soon as he could.

Even still, it took nearly three days of riding before the huge Columbia River came into sight. Barlow had even skirted the Reverend Sterling's mission—where he and Sarah had been married, and where Sarah was now buried. He did not want to deal with the missionary and his wife. They were not his type of people at the best of times, and right now he wanted no distractions, no sermons, nothing to get in his way.

Finally, he and the others crossed the Columbia and rode into the busy Hudson's Bay Company trading post. He stopped at the trade room where his father-in-law could often be found, and went inside, followed, as always, by Buffalo.

"Welcome, son," Stewart said. Despite the lingering grief he felt over the loss of his daughter and two grandchildren, he was glad to see Barlow. He had always liked his son-in-law.

"Thank you, Duncan," Barlow said.

Stewart noticed the almost haunted look in Barlow's eyes and knew something was bothering him. "You have news?" he asked, half in eagerness, half in fear. He knew, of course, that Barlow had been in Umpqua country. Since Anna wasn't with him, then either she was dead or Barlow had some new information on where she might be.

"I do," Barlow said flatly. "The festerin' clam-fuckin' son of a bitch who took Anna wagered her in a game of hand."

"The reprehensible bastard," Stewart said, his Scottish burr thicker than usual.

"That he was," Barlow agreed.

Stewart's eyebrows went up in question.

"He's wolf bait now, ol' hoss." Barlow briefly described what had been done with Red Cedar.

"Och!" Stewart growled. " 'Twas still too good for the likes of him," he said. "Did ye learn where our darlin' Anna is?"

"More or less. She was taken east by a Shoshoni named White Bear."

"Ye are goin' after her, aye?" Stewart asked, eyes narrowed.

"Damn right I am. Ain't nothin' in heaven or on earth that'll stop me, Duncan."

"What're ye doon back here, then, lad? Why did ye nae go after her straight away?"

"Need supplies, Duncan. I figure it's gonna take a spell for me to track this White Bear and his band down. I'm low on powder, shot and damn near everything else."

Stewart nodded. "Of course. Well, ye go on o'er to see Joseph and fill your belly, lad. I'll go aboot settin' aside supplies for ye. And then get yourself a good night's rest. 'Tis near dark, and ye'd be foolish to leave now."

"This here's too important for me to go sittin' on my ass, Duncan," Barlow snapped. "Time's a-wastin'."

"Hell's bells, lad," Stewart snapped back. "If ye canna think of yourself, think of yer animals. Old Beelzebub needs to be watered and fed, and he needs rest. And ye'll be all the more alert with a good night's sleep."

Barlow nodded. "You're right, Duncan." He wasn't happy about it, but he recognized the sense of it.

"Just go eat, lad. You'll feel better after that. I'll see to your supplies."

"I got no cash, Duncan. I was wonderin' if you . . . "

"Don't ye worry aboot that, lad," Stewart said.

"You certain?"

"Aye." His voice left no room for doubt.

Barlow nodded and headed outside. First he took the mule to the blacksmith shop to have him tended. Then he headed for the cook room under McLoughlin's quarters, where Joseph Beaubien held sway. The young French Canadian was a fine cook under any circumstances, but he would put extra effort into his cooking when he liked someone. And he considered Barlow a friend. He thought the same of Buffalo, too, though he had been scared to death of the dog when they had first met.

"Monsieur Barlow," Beaubien said with a wide grin. "*Et* Buffalo! *Bonjour, mes amis! Bonjour!*"

"Howdy, Joseph." Barlow managed a small smile. "You got some vittles for this ol' hoss?"

"*Mais oui!* Always. You sit and rest. I will take care of everything." He turned to an assistant and rattled off a few sharp sentences in French. The assistant ran out, and Beaubien turned to his worktable, where he began preparing food.

The assistant returned minutes later with a bottle of whiskey and a mug. He placed them in front of Barlow and then scurried off.

Barlow sipped whiskey, feeling the tiredness wash over him. The past week had been tough. Lack of sleep and the tenseness of having to deal with the Umpquas under the circumstances that had arisen served to wear him down, and he had not realized it until he relaxed a little. His head began to nod, and he kept jerking himself awake.

Beaubien placed several plates in front of him. The delightful aromas perked Barlow up some. And shoveling in the delicious food served to restore him considerably. He at last sat back, sated, and sipped some coffee laced with whiskey, and puffed a pipe. Buffalo lay nearby, giving a large bone a good going-over.

Finally, Barlow rose and stretched. He looked at the dog, who gazed back, looking quizzical. Barlow almost smiled. "You mind if Buffler stays here with his bone?"

"*Mais non, monsieur.* 'E is most welcome."

"Thank you, Joseph. Jist send him on his way when you git tired of him. He'll find me." Barlow strolled out, heading toward the saloon in a log building at the far end of the fort. Inside, he spotted his five traveling companions, and joined them.

He ordered a mug of whiskey, and when he got it, raised it in a salute to his comrades before draining half of it in one big gulp. He set the mug down and said, "You boys best be gettin' some robe time. I aim to set out come first light."

"Well, we been meanin' to talk to ye about that, Will," Richwine said diffidently. "I don't expect we'll be goin' on with ye."

"Why's that?" Barlow asked evenly, though his anger began to rise.

"We got better things to be doin' than traipsin' after a girl we don't know none," Richwine said with a shrug.

"Ain't a mighty neighborly way of thinkin'," Barlow allowed.

Richwine shrugged. "Don't make us no nevermind. Look, ol' hoss, we signed on with ye last time lookin' for some adventure. Goddamn, but things've been gaw-dawful dull since beaver don't shine no more. We figured ye was headin' down there to that Umpqua land to raise hair on them red devils. Not jist fandango with 'em a wee bit. We aim to find us some more adventurous doin's."

Barlow's tiredness, combined with the anxiety of his daughter's fate as well as his burning desire to get out after Anna, and now rage at his recent companions made him surly. "I didn't figure you boys'd go back on your word."

"Hell, son, we ain't goin' back on our word," Eli Whitfield tossed in. "We give our word to go down to Umpqua country with ye and help ye try'n find that gal of yourn. Well, she weren't there. We done what we said. Now it's time for us to mosey on our own way."

"Besides," Bob Carruthers added, "she weren't but a girl chil' and a half-breed at that. Hell, hoss, find yourself another half-breed woman, or a full-breed Injin and have yourself a passel more of 'em. This one who's missin' won't remember you even if you can find her."

Barlow said nothing while the seconds ticked away as he tried to control the surge of fury that welled up in him. Finally he managed to speak. "I never reckoned you boys to be cowards," he said harshly, glaring at Carruthers.

The big former mountain man's eyes clouded in anger. "Ain't no man ary called me a coward afore and lived through it," he said in low, angry tones.

"You don't like my words, ol' hoss, come on at me," Barlow snapped as he turned to face the big man. "A sack of shit like you don't worry me none."

Carruthers launched a ham-sized fist at Barlow, who jerked back out of the way, and with his left fist smashed Carruthers in the side of the face. Carruthers grunted with the impact, and he slumped onto the bar and then slid to the floor. Barlow stomped on his ribs, and then swung around, just in time to catch a glancing blow off the chin from Richwine.

Barlow snapped an elbow into the nape of Richwine's neck, then half turned and grabbed Mark Aikens, who was charging. Using Aikens's momentum, Barlow bent and pushed up, tossing Aikens over the bar, where he crashed to the floor.

Richwine grabbed Barlow in a bear hug from behind, roaring with anger, but Barlow managed to get his feet planted. With his tree-trunk-like legs providing the power, he thrust backward, slamming Richwine's back against the edge of the bar top. Richwine screeched and released Barlow, who whirled and smashed Richwine in the face several times. Richwine's eyes rolled up and he sank to the floor, unconscious.

Barlow slowly turned and stopped, waiting for Carruthers to get to his feet. Carruthers was the one who had started it all, and most of Barlow's immediate anger was toward him. When Carruthers was on his feet, though still shaky, Barlow stepped up and punched him in the chest, right over the heart.

Carruthers's face lost its color and he gasped, fighting for breath.

"Talk bad about my girl chil', will you, you son of a bitch?" Barlow muttered. "I'll learn you to leave off such doin's." He hammered Carruthers several times in the face and chest, each blow landing with a loud thud and a jolt of satisfaction for Barlow.

Suddenly, however, Barlow was grabbed by several men. Eyes wild, he fought with the ferocity of a cornered wolverine, flinging men left and right. He did this until it finally dawned on him that the men trying to restrain him were not his foes, but some of the men of the fort, who simply wanted to keep him from killing Carruthers.

Not that the fort employees cared if Barlow—a man they knew and liked since he had become one of them to a certain extent—killed a fractious, trouble-causing American like Bob Carruthers. But the Hudson's Bay Company's factor, Dr. John McLoughlin, did not appreciate killing for no good reason.

Once he realized who it was, Barlow quit fighting. The others were wary, continuing to hold him. "Leave off me, dammit," he snapped, jerking his arms free. "I ain't gonna hurt him no more."

He walked back to the bar, using exaggerated motions to avoid stepping on Richwine and Carruthers. He picked up his mug of whiskey and drained it. Then he turned and left, wiping his mouth on a sleeve as he did.

He spent that night with his in-laws in their house a half-mile or so up the Columbia from the fort. Though staying there brought back more vivid memories of Sarah, it was also in some ways comforting. Duncan Stewart and his Chinook wife, whom he called Julia, were a kindly and warm couple, and had taken a liking to Barlow right from the start. Julia was quiet, but she had ways of making Barlow know that he was a welcome visitor in her home.

In the morning, Barlow rode back to the fort with Stewart, Buffalo bounding along beside them. The men were silent, each immersed in their own thoughts. Each had lost the same woman, and each had loved her in his own way. And each knew what Barlow had to do. Stewart wished he could go with his son-in-law, but he could not. He had Julia to consider, and their two other children, as well as his duties at the fort. He was sure Barlow would not want him along anyway. Not in this quest.

Stewart had been true to his word and had supplies set aside for Barlow, so it did not take long to load two mules with the supplies and for Barlow to saddle Beelzebub. Barlow finally climbed onto the animal, and set his rifle across the saddle in front of him. "You've been a big help, Duncan," he said somberly.

"I dinna do hardly anythin'," Stewart responded. "But ye find that little lass of ours, lad. Ye find her and bring her home."

"I aim to, Duncan. It may take me a spell, but I aim to bring that baby girl home." He leaned over to shake Stewart's hand, and then rode out of the fort. Ten minutes later, he was on a ferry across the Columbia. He turned east, heading up the river, following the south bank.

Several weeks later, he rode into Fort Hall, the Hudson's Bay Company post on the Snake River. It was at the northern edge of Shoshoni territory, and Barlow was certain the men there would have some idea of where White Bear's band might be.

He went directly to the factor's office, where his anger and barely contained ferocity gained him entrance. Finan McTavish welcomed him and offered him a seat. With a growl, Barlow took it.

"So, Mr. Barlow, what can I do for ye." His burr was even more pronounced than Stewart's.

"I'm lookin' for a Shoshoni named White Bear. You know where his village would be?"

"Nae, I canna say I do," McTavish said after a few moments' reflection. "I canna say I even know him. What do ye want him for?"

"I hear he has a white child captive," Barlow growled. "My daughter."

"I'm sorry, Mr. Barlow," McTavish said. "I canna help ye."

Barlow wasn't sure he was telling the truth, but he could not prove otherwise, so he simply nodded, valiantly keeping his rage bottled up inside. "Can I get some vittles and a bottle?" he asked. "And maybe a woman?"

"Aye. Talk to my clerk, Mister Buxton. I hope ye dunna have your sights set on anythin' too fancy for eatin'. Our cook is nae the best. And the woman will be a Bannock, most likely." He did not seem apologetic in the least.

Barlow shrugged. "Makes me no nevermind what she is."

McTavish nodded, unconcerned.

4

IAN BUXTON TURNED out to be a prissy, pasty-skinned little Englishman with a blond, pencil-thin mustache and matching Van Dyke beard. Barlow took an instant disliking to him, but had no qualms about asking him where he had to go to find food.

Buxton looked Barlow up and down, appraising the filthy, bulky former trapper. "Food for the likes of you can be had in the small cabin over there," he sniffed. He pointed to a decrepit room in a back corner of the small trading post. I hope you have a strong stomach."

"I've ate my fill of poor food, Mr. Buxton," Barlow said sourly, annoyed at the remembrance, as well as the clerk's attitude. "I reckon I can survive whatever your cook can come up with." He paused. "There whiskey available in there, too?"

"Aye."

Barlow nodded. "And the women? They outside in that little group of lodges just to the south?"

Buxton nodded, disdain written all over his face. "The women are filthy, and Old Man Verhoeven, who runs the operation, is a thief. Be forewarned."

"I'll keep it in mind. Much obliged, Mr. Buxton." He

walked away, gathering his mules and taking them to the stable, where he arranged with the blacksmith to have them tended to. Then, with Buffalo at his side, he headed for the shack that served as a dining hall for the poorer men at the fort.

The cook himself—a profane, surly man with a sour attitude and slovenly manners—served Barlow, slapping plates and bowls of almost undefinable foodstuffs down on the table. As he turned to leave, Barlow said, "Whiskey."

"You too good to drink coffee, hoss?" the cook asked with a larger snarl than usual.

"Nope," Barlow said just as cantankerously, "I jist need somethin' to help ease down this slop you're tryin' to foist off as food. Now fetch me a bottle and keep your goddamn trap shut."

The cook did as he was told, but made his greater-than-usual irritation known by slamming the whiskey bottle on the wood table and stomping off muttering obscenities to himself.

Barlow did not bother with the tin mug the cook had also brought. He simply tilted the bottle up to his mouth and drained a fair amount. He managed not to sputter—it was the most foul-tasting concoction being passed for whiskey that he had ever poured into his gullet. But it was ambrosia compared with the swill served up as food. Barlow never did figure out what it was, though if he had had to venture a guess, he might have said it had started out as some form of antelope stew. Barlow managed to get down two full bowls of the stuff, and part of another. Buffalo ate some, too, though the dog didn't seem all that eager for it.

Still, as poor as it was, the meal filled the hole in his stomach, and for that Barlow was grateful. He just hoped the repast would stay down.

Finished eating, Barlow chanced the coffee, which to his surprise was quite tasty. It was better than what he usually made himself, though it could not compare with Sarah's. Done with that and a pipe, Barlow walked back to the blacksmith shop, and borrowed a horse, letting Beelzebub stay where he was and rest. He rode out of the fort, heading for the cluster of tipis less than a quarter of a mile from the fort. He dismounted and tied the horse to a tree, and approached a man who had come out of a lodge and was standing there, hands across his chest.

"You Old Man Verhoeven?" Barlow asked.

"Yah. Vhat can I do for you?"

Barlow looked at the man in disgust. He was so foul-looking as to make the cook appear to be the prissy Buxton's better. "What in hell do you think I'm here for, you damn fool?"

"Fifty cent'," Verhoeven said, apparently not offended by Barlow's tone.

"How much for all night?"

"Five dollars."

"Mr. Buxton was right, boy. You are a goddamn thief." He turned and headed toward the horse.

"Vait!" Verhoeven said, hurrying after him.

Barlow stopped and turned to face the fetid reprobate.

"For you, only four dollars."

"Two dollars and not a goddamn penny more, you goddamn pirate."

"Dot is robbery," Verhoeven said. "If you von't pay vhat I asked, you can go somevhere else." There was, of course, nowhere else to go.

Barlow's already poor mood worsened. "I am in no humor for takin' any shit from the likes of you."

Verhoeven glared at him with piggish eyes set in a fat, florid face. Keeping his stare on Barlow, he called out, "Hans!"

Barlow glanced up to see a mountain walking toward him. Hans was fully half a foot taller than Barlow, and outweighed him by sixty pounds. Not that Barlow was worried. He grew even less worried as Hans got closer. Much of that sixty extra pounds was flab.

"Yah, Papa?" Hans asked, stopping next to Verhoeven.

"This gentleman does not vish to abide by my rules. Encourage him to change his mind. Or to leaf."

"Yah." Hans turned and took two steps toward Barlow, and was promptly knocked on his ass by the former mountain man's powerful right fist.

Hans rose slowly, shaking his head. He had never been hit so hard, though a good many men had tried to knock him down. "Dot vas a mistake," he growled as his head began to clear.

Barlow shrugged. "Look, boy, I came here for a woman, not to fight a bloated sack of shit who don't know any manners because his lard-ass father never taught him any. If you come at me again, ol' hoss, ye'll get a heap more than a knockin' down."

"Papa?" Hans asked over his shoulder. He was eager to take this man on now. He realized he should've been prepared the first time. He wouldn't make that mistake again.

"Break him," Verhoeven snarled.

Hans moved forward, alert, ready, arms spread, his fingers ready to grab Barlow and choke the life out of him. He swung a mighty right fist at Barlow's face. It was fast, darting, designed to disable a man instantly. Except that this time it hit nothing but air. Hans had never seen anyone move that fast.

The fist sailed within an inch of Barlow's jaw, and when it was passed, he grabbed Hans's arm in both hands, one at the wrist, the other at the tricep. And he twisted the arm up and back.

Hans's momentum played into Barlow's hands, and he found himself with one cheek flattened on the ground, searing pain running through his arm, and Barlow's foot on his back holding him down. He was helpless. Any move he made would leave him with an arm and shoulder that might be crippled for life.

"Two dollars?" Barlow asked.

Verhoeven sighed, as if greatly put upon. "You drife a hard bargain, Mister," he said. He paused, and then nodded, "Deal. Now let mein boy up."

"In a bit. I want the best you got."

"Dot vould be Gretchen. Or Eva."

Barlow was suspicious. Verhoeven had answered mighty quickly. Barlow twisted the young man's shoulder some more, and Hans screamed as ligaments tore in his arm and shoulder.

"All right!" Verhoeven said, worry creasing his fat face. "Beatrix is the best I haf. She is a Bannock. Very pretty. Very willing. Dot's her lodge there, vit the sun painted on it."

Barlow nodded and let Hans's arm go. He looked at Verhoeven. "The next time you send someone to do me harm, hoss, I'll kill him. And then you. Understand?"

"Yah," Verhoeven said sourly.

With Buffalo at his side, Barlow strode toward the lodge. A young Bannock woman, attractive at this distance, waited outside, watching. She was smiling a little. After all, anyone who could manhandle Hans Verhoeven so easily had to be someone special. She might even enjoy this one.

Her smile faltered a little when she saw the hard light in his eyes, but she plastered it back on. He was, after all, a customer, and if she was to get her piddling salary from Verhoeven, she would have to at least pretend to be almost happy.

"How you want this?" she asked.

"Ever' which way you can think of, girl," Barlow responded. "And as many ways as this ol' hoss can manage." He almost managed a smile.

"Well, then," Beatrix said, quietly, back in her element, "let's shuck these clothes." She swiftly, with practiced ease, divested herself of her white women's dress.

Barlow pulled off his cloth shirt and dropped it. Beatrix gasped softly when she saw his broad, wound-scarred chest.

"Somethin' wrong?" he asked.

"No. Nothing wrong." She couldn't help but stare, though. She had never seen the likes of this man before. He was as broad as he was tall, or so he seemed, and precious little of that width was fat. Moments later when he dropped his pants, she was even more impressed.

Beatrix laid down on the pile of buffalo hides and blankets that served as her bed, her legs spread, her womanhood open and waiting for him. She smiled her encouragement. She was rather surprised that when he knelt between her legs he did not just punch himself into her. Instead, he leaned forward, holding himself up on his big powerful arms, and then dipped his head until his teeth latched on to one nipple. He bit gently and tugged at it before letting the succulent piece of woman flesh pop out of his mouth. He then tongued the nipple into wet hardness, sucking it in and letting it slide out. He soon moved on to the other breast and performed the same pleasurable actions there.

Beatrix wriggled a little. Then more. As she did, her womanhood encountered the tip of Barlow's lance. She gasped, and suddenly found herself wanting this huge, muscular man. She had not felt this way in ages. Most of the men she encountered were not concerned about her in the least; they simply wanted to jam their pizzles into her and thrust a few times before spilling their seed in her, and then they would slink away, almost ashamed, only to brag later over some whiskey with other men who had done the same thing. But this man was a whole different species, and she could not believe her luck. She suddenly was determined to enjoy it as much as possible.

Hearing her moans, and taking note of the squirming she was doing, Barlow pulled his head back and grinned a little. "Like that, do you, Miss Beatrix?"

"Oh, yes, Mister . . . ?" she looked puzzled, but then she didn't really care that she did not know his name. "Mister."

"Call me Will," he said before turning his attentions back to her breasts. He wanted to continue this for a while, but he had been without a woman for a long time, and he could not wait. Besides, she seemed close to reaching her peak. "You ready?" he asked, voice harsh with lust.

"Yes," she gasped. "Yes, yes!" She reached down with a small hand, grabbed his hard shaft and guided it into her. She sighed as he pushed himself hard, deep, deep into her.

He rested there for a moment, buried all the way to the root in her velvety, soft love canal. Then, still holding himself up with his powerful arms, he began thrusting in and out of her, setting a smooth, slow rhythm that soon increased and then more.

Beatrix suddenly shrieked and bucked like a cat walking across hot coals. Barlow picked up the pace until he reached his own peak moments later. With an animal-like grunt and a howl, he released his fluid into her.

Now weak, he pulled out of Beatrix and flopped onto his back next to her, breathing hard.

Beatrix rose up on an elbow and peered at his face. "You mighty damn good," she said with a big grin.

"Oh, you think so, eh?" Barlow gasped, smiling a little himself.

"I do," Beatrix said with a firm nod. "Ain't many men like you, you know."

"Thank you," Barlow said quietly, not knowing what else to say. "You mind if I get a little shut-eye? I reckon we can have us another little shivaree right after."

"No mind. You gonna stay a while?"

"The night, if you got no objections."

"None. You rest. I go get some food. If Old Man lets me."

"He gives you any trouble, come and git me. Or jist tell him that if I have to git up and go on out there, I'm gonna gut him and his pig-faced son."

Beatrix giggled. She actually wouldn't mind seeing that, considering how the Verhoevens treated her. She rose and tugged on her dress. Suddenly a questioning look flickered across her face. "What about your dog?" she asked. "He gonna let me back in here?"

"Yep. Jist pet him when you come in. And maybe

toss him some meat scraps or something. His name's
Buffler."

Barlow neither knew nor cared what time it was when
he woke. He felt refreshed, and his humor was even
better, though it was never great these days. Nor would
it be until he found Anna.

"Food's ready," Beatrix said. "You hungry?"

"Very." He took the plate of buffalo meat and wolfed
it down, then asked for more. He polished that off, too,
and two cups of coffee. Done, he wiped his hands on
his cloth shirt, which was laying nearby. He had not
bothered to get dressed.

"Now," he said with an almost impudent grin, "I'm
hungry for somethin' else, woman."

With a gleam of lust in her eyes, Beatrix quickly
stripped down again under Barlow's watchful, interested
eyes. Moments later, they were entwined together in the
robes, as Barlow stroked Beatrix's body until she was
panting and moaning, and almost begging him to take
her. But he refused. "Not just yet," he said quietly, enjoying his power over the young woman.

Barlow's hand cupped Beatrix's sopping love mound,
exciting both of them, and then slipped a big finger into
her. He alternated wriggling his finger inside her and
teasing her love button, and soon she was screaming as
she peaked.

Barlow kept up his manipulations, until she squealed
with another orgasm, her silken womanhood grasping
his finger tightly.

After several more of those, he rolled her over so she
was on her stomach and then tugged her hips until she
lifted her backside up to him. He knelt between her legs
behind her. With a swift, sure stroke, he plunged his
lance into her as far as it would go. She gasped, and
then moaned in ecstasy as her silky passage adjusted
easily to accommodate him.

Barlow grabbed her wide, dusky hips with his hands

and then thundered in and out of her, his testicles slapping her fleshy mound.

Beatrix was moaning almost constantly, the low sounds punctuated by screeches of joy as climax after climax rippled through her one after another, each more powerful than the last.

Finally Barlow bellowed, and flooded her insides with his essence. His back arched and his neck stretched as he sucked in air through gritted teeth. Minutes later, he collapsed on the robes.

5

WILL BARLOW RODE out of Fort Hall in a foul, angry humor. He had spent a fine night with Beatrix, but this morning had been a total waste. He had gone around the fort, talking to anyone who would give him a few minutes of their time, asking about the Shoshonis and where a warrior named White Bear might be found. No one knew anything. Or, if they did, they were not telling Barlow about it. The only response other than a flat-out "No" he got was from O'Day, the blacksmith, who before he spoke looked around as if afraid someone might be listening.

"All I can tell you, Mr. Barlow," O'Day said nervously, "is that I ain't ever heard of a Shoshoni named White Bear. And I been here some years."

"Never have, eh?" Barlow questioned. He was certain the man was lying. But there was nothing he could do about it.

"That's a fact. You sure it was a Shoshoni took your girl?"

"About as sure of it as I can be, which ain't all that much," Barlow admitted. For all he knew, Red Cedar could've been lying as much as Barlow figured O'Day

was. But it was all he had to go on, and he had to believe
in it.

"I think that maybe whoever told you that was not
tellin' true, Mister."

"No more than you," Barlow thought. Aloud he said,
"Could be. But I reckon I got to find out for myself."
In disgust, he set about loading his pack mules, saddled
Beelzebub and rode out, Buffalo loping happily in front,
to the side or behind, as was his wont at any particular
moment.

As he rode past the tipi brothel, he tipped his hat to
Beatrix, and grinned rudely at the Verhoevens, who
grimaced at him. Suddenly Barlow stopped and turned
back. He stopped again right by the Verhoevens. "If I
ever hear you've harmed Beatrix," he said harshly, with
no preliminary, "I'll be back to carve you into bits so
small even a starvin' buzzard wouldn't bother himself
with 'em. That clear to you?"

Neither man said anything, they just stared sullenly at
Barlow.

"You two as deaf as you are stupid?" Barlow asked
with a sneer.

"Ve understand," Old Man Verhoeven growled petu-
lantly.

"Jist keep it in mind." He turned the mule's head with
the reins and rode slowly off, his temper not assuaged
any. He was disgusted with everything concerned with
his search—from the lack of information to the poor
attitudes of others to the seeming futility of it. But he
had no give-up in him over the matter. He had nothing
else in life to do other than look for little Anna. He had
no ties to anyone, to any place. He had no real home,
not even any real friends. He was as free as a man could
be to pursue his quest.

Because of that, he felt no loneliness on the long,
wearying trail. Well, not the loneliness of being on his
own. The loneliness of all he had lost was another story.
Thoughts of Sarah were always with him. As were
thoughts of Anna. She would be three now, and growing

more aware. He only hoped that she would remember him when he found her. Until he did find her, he would ride with the heaviness of loss weighing on him.

He traveled slowly. There was no reason to hurry when he had no real idea of where he had to go. The Shoshonis were a nomadic tribe and covered a lot of ground, particularly during the summer, when they would do a lot of visiting amongst their own bands, as well as far away to old ancestral kin such as the Comanches. Which meant that villages could be anywhere, and all he could do was ride and look for them. So he did. As he traveled, his eyes constantly scanned the surroundings, always on the alert for any sign of a Shoshoni village.

Within a week, he had found two villages. He had dealt with the Shoshonis before, and had always known them to be reasonably friendly to the white man, so instead of sneaking around, he simply rode slowly toward each village when he saw it. As was often the case with tribes out here in the Rockies, and on the Plains, a group of warriors raced out to confront him as soon as they became aware of him.

With signs, English and a little Shoshoni that he had picked up years ago in his mountain days, he explained that he was just traveling through and would be happy to trade a little for some furs, and for a place to stay for the night. Both times he was taken into the village and welcomed. He did a little trading, and casually asked about a warrior named White Bear or if anyone had seen a captive white girl among the other bands.

He had no more luck with the people of these two villages, however, than he had had in Fort Hall. No one had ever heard of White Bear or knew of a captive white girl.

"We friends to white-eyes," one warrior said to him as they ate antelope stew one evening. "We not take white girl captive."

"I know you didn't take her captive, Black Lance," Barlow answered, trying to stay calm. "I said she was won while wagering with some Umpquas, far to the west, where the big water is."

Black Lance nodded. "If we find her, we give her back to the white-eyes. We friends to the white-eyes."

"Yep, I know," Barlow said with a sigh, his exasperation fading into despair.

But nothing would deter him, and the next morning he rode out of the village with renewed determination, if not any better humor. A few weeks later, he spotted another village, and his hopes rose minutely again. He had seen enough failure that he would not allow his hopes to get too high, but he could not help them rising some whenever he encountered a village, as there was always a chance that Anna would be there.

He realized at the last moment, when a phalanx of warriors surrounded him, that they were not Shoshonis—they were Northern Paiutes. He did not know them well, and was not sure how he would be treated by them. He explained with signs that he was just passing through and would like to trade a little. The warriors seemed to accept that and led him to the village.

He was treated well enough, and soon he was sitting with some warriors around a fire outside the lodge of a civil chief named Yellow Blanket. Barlow thought he detected some of the men—and women—looking covetously at Buffalo, but he tried to ignore it. They would not try anything with him sitting right there, even if Buffalo would allow one of the Paiutes to get close to him. As usual, the great Newfoundland lay at Barlow's side, resting, but ears and nose twitching as he kept alert to any danger.

The Paiutes and Barlow ate bowls of something that Barlow couldn't identify but which he didn't think tasted too bad. Soon they traded a little, though no one really had his heart in it, since neither side really had much to offer. Finally, the talk, all in signs with a dash of English thrown in now and again, turned to general things.

Barlow decided it was as good a time as any to bring up the subject of his quest. In signs he asked, "Do you know of a Shoshoni named White Bear? Or a white girl captive of the Shoshonis?"

The Paiutes' attitude shifted suddenly to an iciness bred of distrust and perhaps even a little hatred. It startled Barlow, who immediately concluded that he had touched a nerve. But he had no time right now to ponder its significance. All his senses were heightened because of the increased tension in the air around him, and he expected an attack at any moment.

None came, and he relaxed a little after several minutes. Yellow Blanket finally said in signs, "We know of no one named White Bear. Nor of any white captives. We have no captives. We are friendly to the whites. Always."

Barlow nodded. He was sure the Paiute was lying, but he didn't know whether it was just about some of it or all of it. He was certain that they had no captives in the village. Or else they were hiding them very well. And he had no reason to believe that they had Anna here. Unless Red Cedar had lied when he said that White Bear was a Shoshoni. Maybe White Bear really was a Northern Paiute, which was why Yellow Blanket and his warriors had gotten so cold all of a sudden when he had asked his question.

They all broke up soon after, the Paiutes heading for their lodges, Barlow to a spot he had picked out earlier as a good place to spend the night. So as not to raise any suspicions, he unsaddled Beelzebub, though he did leave the pack mules loaded.

Several hours later, when the camp was asleep, Barlow rose and quietly saddled Beelzebub. Moving slowly so he didn't disrupt the peacefulness of the village's slumber, he walked out of the camp, leading Beelzebub and the two pack mules. Buffalo padded quietly beside him.

Half a mile outside of the village, Barlow climbed up onto the mule and rode off. The three-quarter moon and the many stars gave him plenty of light to travel by, but he moved slowly. While there was enough light for traveling, there were still a lot of hazards that could not be seen. Besides, he was in no rush. He would be a few miles from the Northern Paiute village by daylight, and he doubted they would come after him. They had no reason to, as far as he could determine. He just wanted out of the village because they might have tried something against him there simply because it was convenient.

There was little out here, so he had to ride until more than an hour after daybreak before he found a spot that would afford him at least a little shelter from the sweltering sun. It wasn't much, but the small stand of scrubby, wind-twisted trees surrounding an almost invisible water hole would have to do. Barlow unsaddled Beelzebub and unloaded the supplies from the two pack mules. He tended the animals perfunctorily and then dug in the sand a little until he had enough water to fill his small coffeepot. He set that on a small fire and chewed some jerky while he waited for the coffee to be ready.

Buffalo trotted off, and returned just as Barlow was pouring himself some coffee, with a huge jackrabbit clutched in his powerful jaws. He lay down near the fire and proceeded to wolf down his recently caught meal.

"Ain't you even gonna share with me, you damn dog?" Barlow said with something approaching a chuckle.

The Newfoundland looked at him balefully and went back to feeding.

"Well, hell, I wouldn't share with me either, ol' hoss," Barlow said. He sipped his coffee and puffed a pipe. When he was done, he dug at the water hole a little more so there was enough there for the dog and the mules to drink their fill, though it would take them a while.

Finally he stretched out, head on his saddle, and pulled his slouch hat down over his eyes. He was asleep in seconds.

A low growl from Buffalo woke Barlow. He shoved his hat back and looked around without moving. "What is it, boy?" he asked the dog. "We got company come callin'?"

Barlow rolled over onto his stomach and then squirmed back to the saddle. He laid his rifle across it, after making sure it was ready to fire. He waited. Suddenly an Indian popped up less than ten feet away, and charged.

Barlow barely had time to fire, but he did. The ball caught the warrior—one of the Northern Paiutes who had been at the fire with him last night—square in the chest and flattened him.

Barlow grabbed the two big, single-shot caplock pistols from the saddle holsters and then rolled over and over until he was behind one of the scrawny, deformed trees.

Four warriors suddenly appeared, seemingly out of nowhere, having found some way to sneak up despite there being nothing much in the landscape to hide behind. They all charged, from various angles.

Barlow fired both pistols. The ball from one hit a warrior, who crashed to the ground in a jumble of arms and legs that suddenly did not work. Barlow's other shot missed, and he threw the pistol at another of the charging warriors. He ducked and a stone war club just missed mashing his head. He half spun and slammed the back of his upper arm against the throat of the Indian who had just taken a swing at him. The warrior dropped like a stone, gurgling sounds struggling weakly from his mangled throat.

Buffalo charged at the warrior whom Barlow had fired at and missed. The big dog leaped onto the Indian's chest, knocking him to the ground. The Newfoundland tore at the screeching warrior's neck, ripping out chunks of flesh as the Indian tried to hit the Newfoundland with his war club. But he had little leverage, and the dog did so much damage so fast that the Indian could put only a little strength into the blows, which swiftly became more and more feeble, and then stopped.

Barlow turned toward the fourth warrior, but he was

having no more of this particular battle. He had helped up the comrade whom Barlow had flattened with his arm, and the two of them were fleeing across the scrubby desert land. "Buffler," he called sharply, "leave him be now."

The dog reluctantly backed away from the mangled warrior and went off to lick the blood off his chops.

Barlow wondered what to do. He wanted—needed—more sleep, and he was sure he would be left alone for a while. On the other hand, he had no desire to lay here trying to sleep with three corpses around him and he was too damned tired and lazy to drag them out of sight. He also thought that if he rode out soon, the others might return to get the bodies of their friends, and if they found them unmutilated, unscalped, they might just leave Barlow in peace if he ever saw them again. He finally decided that would be the best thing. He drank some coffee and ate some jerky as he loaded the pack mules and saddled his mount. Soon he was pulling out, Buffalo trotting proudly along.

He headed east for some days and then started angling toward the north once he had hit the mountains. He had a vague notion of getting back to Fort Hall to restock on supplies—if he could find some money, or talk someone there into lending him some. He would worry about that when he got there, since it was still some distance away.

It had been more than a month and a half since he had left Fort Hall when he crested a grassy ridge and saw a lone wagon traveling across the valley below. A wagon with no men around that he could see. And, despite his determination to continue his quest, his good side rose up and forced him to go see just what had brought these women out here with a wagon and no menfolk. He was pretty certain it would not be a good story.

A couple of hours later, he was sitting at a fire with three women—one young, not yet out of her teens, and

very pretty; one who was obviously the young woman's
mother, who in her thirties, perhaps, and not unattractive; and an older woman who still looked good—waiting for them to tell their tale.

6

"WE WERE HEADING for the Oregon country with a few other wagons, Mister Barlow," the eldest woman, Hope Skinner, said. "Somewhere along the way, my husband, Simon, in his infinite wisdom, decided to try a different route. Said he'd heard about it from some old mountain man back along the trail somewhere. It was supposed to cut many miles off our trip, saving the oxen."

"He was lied to," Barlow said flatly.

"We realized that after a spell, Mister Barlow," Hope said, shaking her head sadly. "But Mister Skinner was a stubborn man, and was not about to turn back." She paused. "There was trouble even before we left, however—Judith's husband, Sam, decided to stay with the other wagons," she said, pointing to the youngest woman. "He tried to talk her into staying, too, but she would have none of it." Hope seemed mighty proud of her granddaughter's rebelliousness. "Especially after learning that his head had been turned by a young woman with one of the other wagons." A look of distaste covered her face.

Barlow looked at the woman, a little surprised to see

that she was not that bad looking. He didn't think she
was even fifty yet, though a life of toil, and likely some
strife if her indications that her husband was so hard-
headed were true, had aged her some. However, he could
still see the beauty of her youth beneath the creases on
her face. She was relatively tall for a woman, and somewhat thin. Her hair was mixed about half and half with
a chestnut brown and a shiny gray, and her eyes were
determined.

"Sounds like a damn fool to me," Barlow said, glancing at the young Judith. She was seventeen or eighteen
and had a lithe, sweet grace about her. But he could see
her grandmother's determination in her sparkling eyes
and in the firm set of her full lips. Like her grandmother,
she was taller than most women, and her figure was
womanly and well rounded. His thoughts about her flickered on the carnal before he managed to bring his mind
back to Hope, who was speaking again.

"Darn tootin' he's a fool," Hope said. "Worse even
than my Simon. At least Mister Skinner's foolishness
did not involve other women."

"So what happened then?" Barlow prompted. He did
not relish getting into an argument over the foibles of
men, particularly men he had never met. He had felt
comfortable speaking poorly of Judith's husband, because any man who left a sweet, strong young woman
who was as beautiful as Judith Dockery was had to be
a prime fool. But much beyond that comment, he was
not willing to go.

"After some days—maybe a week—of wanderin', we
realized we were lost out here in this harsh wilderness,"
Hope continued. "We spotted a small camp of Indians.
We thought they were Shoshonis, whom we had heard
were friendly to whites, so we headed there to seek their
help." She paused and sighed, a shudder rippling
through her shoulders. But she firmed them and went
on. "Instead, Mister Barlow, the Injins attacked us, killin' Mister Skinner. With me and Judith helping Cora's
husband—my son, George, and Cora watching over the

young'ns as best she could, we managed to drive the demons off." Her voice caught in her throat. "But not before those savages run off with two of our young'ns—Judith's youngest, Sam Junior, and Cora's son, Georgie."

Barlow said nothing for a while; he simply sat and let the anger that had suddenly bubbled up inside of him settle some. The thought of Indians stealing more children tore at his heart. Even if these people had been damn fools for having come this way, alone, they did not deserve to be preyed on by fractious warriors.

"You sure they was Shoshonis?" he finally asked.

Hope shrugged. "We were told back in the Settlements that this was Shoshoni country," she said. "We assumed at the time of the attack that they were Shoshonis, and we, of course, have no knowledge to say differently now."

"It's not usual at all for the Snakes, as the Shoshoni are sometimes called, to attack whites. I ain't ever heard the like."

"If they're so good to white folks, why are they called Snakes?" Cora asked.

"Couple reasons, ma'am. The sign in sign language for them is like this." He moved his hand downward in front of him in the image of a snake. "Plus many of them live near the Snake River."

"Oh." Cora didn't seem mollified, but she said nothing more.

"Can you tell me anything of the way these warriors looked?" Barlow asked.

Hope shrugged again. "They looked like Indians, Mister Barlow. Just savage, heathen Indians bent on killin' and destruction. And all of 'em pretty much looked alike."

"How'd they ride? Well? Poorly? Did they sit their ponies like they belonged there? Did they ride proud?"

"Well," Hope said thoughtfully, "I ain't sure—we was a mite occupied at the time, you understand—but I don't think they rode very well. We'd heard that most of the Indians out this way, savages though they might be,

could ride like the devil himself. But these savage certainly didn't seem all that comfortable on their horses."

Barlow nodded. "I'd wager they weren't Shoshonis.
The Snakes ain't the horsemen the Sioux or Crow or
Blackfoot are, but they're better than some others I
know."

"You think you know who these Indians were?" Hope
asked, eyes wide. She didn't know why it was important
to her, it just was.

"Sounds like Northern Paiutes from the little you
could tell me about 'em. But I can't be sure. Not that it
really matters now, I reckon."

"Somehow I think it does," Hope said, "though I can't
for the life of me think of why. Maybe just that when
George gets back with some help, it might help to find
our two lost young'ns."

"Help?" Barlow was a little confused.

"Yes, Mister Barlow. My son George set out on
horseback the day after the attack, hoping to find help.
We had heard that Fort Hall was somewhere to the north
of here, so that's the way he headed. He hoped to get
there and find some help to go out looking for the
young'ns, as well as rescue us."

"I just come from Fort Hall mayhap a month, month
and a half ago, and no one had been there with such a
tale at that time. Nor have I seen anyone during my
travels since." He paused when he saw the fright in the
women's eyes. "But that don't mean much, ladies," he
hurriedly added. "I were travelin' a mighty meanderin'
path. I only come 'cross you folks by fortune. This
here's a mighty big land, and could be hundreds of folks
passing through never see each other."

"I can believe that last part, Mister Barlow," Hope
said, trying to keep the fear out of her voice. "I've never
seen the like of such a wide and wild place."

"It's both of those things, certain, ma'am," Barlow
said in reassuring tones. "I meant no fright to you when
I said I hadn't seen Mister Skinner. I only meant to

imply that he and I probably covered some of the same ground but at different times."

"I understand, Mister Barlow," Hope said.

Barlow nodded. "And what were you women supposed to be doin' while Mister Skinner went traipsin' off lookin' for help?"

"Travelin' as best we could westward and north. Hopefully we would get to Fort Hall, too, or that a search party from there would find us first."

"Why in hell didn't your son stay with you?" Barlow asked, trying to keep the harshness out of his voice. "At least he would have provided you some protection out here if those red devils chose to make another go at you."

"Well, Mister Barlow, it should be obvious to a man like you that he could make much better time on horseback than he could traipsin' along with this ponderous old wagon."

"That he could," Barlow agreed. "But it puts him out there by himself, where he is in terrible danger. From all you've said, he is not used to the ways of the mountains and its inhabitants. There are some savage critters out here, as you've learned so terribly. And it leaves you women without as much protection."

"All that is true, Mr. Barlow," Hope said. "But we thought that the lesser of dangers. Besides," she added with a wan smile, "George has much of his father's rashness running in his blood. He had determined that this was the best course, and he would not be swayed."

Barlow nodded. He had figured that something like that was the case. The menfolk of this little expedition had exhibited nothing but foolishness. "Well," he said after a few moments, "I'll stay the night here with you, if you don't object."

"We'd be pleased to have you, Mr. Barlow," Hope said. Her daughter-in-law and granddaughter nodded. They seemed relieved.

"May I ask you something, Mister Barlow?" Judith questioned.

"Ask away."

"What brings you out here to this godforsaken country? You don't seem to have very many goods, as if you were a trader, nor the supplies that would show you to be a hunter. And I can see no other profession one might carry on out here where there is nothing."

"I'm on a quest, ma'am," Barlow said flatly. He paused, the pain welling up in his heart as it always did when he thought of Anna. "My daughter was took by savages, too," he finally said. "By a band of red devils called Umpquas. Way out in Oregon country. When I found the one who done it, he was persuaded to tell me where she was. The son of a bi—pardon me, ladies . . . the ol' devil told me he lost her in a gambling game to a Shoshoni. I'm out here lookin' for her. Been doin' so for more than a month now." He stopped abruptly, thinking he had already said too much. It was not like him to go into detail about this.

The women looked horror-stricken. They knew what it was like to have lost children to Indians. And they were proud of him for having continued his quest for his daughter. He was the kind of man they all wanted to have, one they could trust and depend on when times were hard.

They sat quietly after that, each with his or her own thoughts, and soon they all headed toward their beds—the women and children under the wagon, Barlow off to the side a little way to give the women privacy. It was too hot for the otter skin robe, but he rested on it, thankful for its softness and the protection it offered from the hard ground.

As they were finishing their meal the next morning, Barlow asked, "Is there anything I can do for you ladies before I ride on?"

"Ride on?" Judith asked, surprised and suddenly frightened.

"Yes'm. I still got to find my Anna."

"We were . . ." Hope started. "We had hoped . . . um, we had talked about the . . . well . . ."

"Jist come out with it, ma'am," Barlow said. He had a feeling he knew what was coming, and he wanted it out in the open so it could be addressed.

Hope composed herself, set her coffee cup down and looked Barlow straight in the eye. "I'm not a woman to beat around the bush, Mister Barlow," she said firmly, all doubts gone. "We are—all of us here—frightened beyond belief. We see hostile savages behind every rock and tree. Last night was the first decent night's sleep we've had since those devils attacked us." She paused, staring at him, trying to gauge his thoughts, but she could not. "We beg you, Mister Barlow, take us to safety. Lead us to Fort Hall."

"I don't know, ma'am," he said. Barlow was torn—he wanted nothing more in life than to find Anna, and he had thought for weeks now, or at least tried to convince himself, that he might be close. He was deep in Shoshoni territory. On the other hand, he couldn't in good conscience leave these women and children out here alone at the mercy of the elements, animals or hostile Indians. Not after all they had already been through.

"You said yourself, it's dangerous for a man traveling alone out here," Hope pressed.

Barlow almost smiled. "I did say that, yes, but I meant that it was dangerous out here for a man who's not used to this country—like your son. I've been ridin' this country for a long spell. Was a mountain man for quite a time back before the beaver trade died out. And I believe you know that was my meanin' when I said it."

"I did," Hope agreed firmly, not backing down a bit. "But I still believe you'd agree that travelin' alone out here is not wise, if it's not necessary."

"Reckon you've got me on that one, ma'am," Barlow said with a nod.

"But more to the point, you said that we should not be travelin' without a man. We are no match for the savages should they return. And, as you say, you are well-versed in the ways of these lands and the savages. You would know if an attack was near. You would know a better route for us to travel to safety. You would . . ."

"All that's true, ma'am," Barlow interjected. "But I got my daughter to think of."

"And we have our young'ns to think of, Mister Barlow," Hope said sharply. "Both those still with us and those who were took by the red demons."

Barlow nodded. "I agree, ma'am. But you were doin' fine before I come along. You'll do fine once I ride on. I'll give you directions on the best way to go. You'll make out."

"Do you seriously think we'll reach Fort Hall by ourselves?" Hope demanded.

He didn't need to answer that. They had less chance of surviving the trek than he seemed to have of finding Anna at the rate he was going.

"You see?" Hope said, proud of her reasoning. "You can't answer. You know the truth of it as well as all of us do. We wouldn't give up—we're not that kind of people, Mister Barlow. But truth be told, ain't none of us has any certainty that we'll get to succor. If the savages don't finish off the job they started, there are the elements. The sun has been torture on us, as you might well imagine. And there are other hardships. Without a certainty of direction, we may wander endlessly while our food runs low and then disappears. Our oxen could perish. Yes, these things could happen even if you are along, but, truly, you must know that we would have a much better chance of survival if you are with us."

He was wavering, and then little Elizabeth—Judith's almost three-year-old—poked her head out from behind her mother's skirts. Barlow's heart constricted when he saw the blonde-haired little girl, and he had no choice. He had to do as they asked. Reluctantly he agreed.

7

BARLOW CHAFED AT the interminable pace at which they had to travel. It galled on him to plod along at such a deadly slow tempo, the screech of the wagon wheels ringing constantly in his ears. Within two days he knew he had to do something. So he began to ride out each day after the morning meal, mounted on Beelzebub, with Buffalo accompanying him. His two pack mules were tied to the back of the sluggishly moving wagon. He would range far and wide, making use of the time and travel. He was always alert to Indian sign, both as a precaution against another attack on the wagon, and for hints of a village where he could look for Anna—or for the two missing children of the emigrants. He also hunted while he was out there, keeping the travelers in fresh meat, which suited him better, and helped the women. They needed their strength for the arduous trek they still faced, and meat would supply that, and it would help stretch their supplies.

A week after Barlow had joined the women, he picked up sign of Indians. He couldn't tell at first whether it was a hunting party or a war party, and he was determined to find out. He rode a little faster, eyes scanning

the ground and horizon alternately, constantly looking
for an indication. Two hours later, he spotted several
horses at a small copse of willows. He stopped, pulled
out a spyglass and looked over the gathering. "Shit," he
muttered. It was a war party, and worse, the warriors
were resting in a spot that the wagon would ride right
by. He turned the mule and said quietly, "C'mon, Buffler, we best make tracks." He trotted off, the Newfoundland keeping pace.

Barlow rode in a direction which he hoped would
bring him to the wagon sufficiently southeast of the
copse that they could give the place a wide berth. But
he misjudged either where he had been when he spotted
the Indians—Northern Paiutes as best as he could tell—
or the speed at which the wagon was traveling. Or perhaps both. Whatever, it was, he cut the trail of the wagon
well southeast of where he had wanted to. They were,
he was afraid, getting mighty close to that copse.

"Goddammit," he snapped, angry at himself. "Buffler,
you catch up the best you can, boy. Me and Beelzebub
got to ride." He slapped the mule's rump with his hat,
and the animal bolted forward. Buffalo kept up for a few
yards but then began to fall back. Barlow did not worry
about him. The dog would not be too far behind.

Barlow could hear the screeching wagon when he was
still almost a mile behind it. He kicked the mule a few
times with his heels, urging even more speed out of the
big beast. Minutes later he spotted the wagon ahead. He
did some quick calculating in his head, hoping he didn't
make the mistakes he had made before when he had set
out to warn the wagon. But if his figuring was accurate,
it was less than half a mile from the copse. If the Indians
were still there, they could not help but hear the thing,
and would certainly be on their way to investigate.

Something had caught the women's attention, and
they had turned to see Barlow racing toward them. They
had halted the wagon and were waiting for him.

He pulled the blowing, sweating mule to a stop amid
a cloud of dust. "There's a small passel of Injins up

ahead, maybe half a mile, and they're painted."

The women and children blanched at the news.

"Unless they rode off a bit ago, I expect they'll be payin' us a visit right soon." He was glad their travel, as slow as it had been, had brought them into a more wooded country. "Let's get the wagon and animals in them trees yonder. Miss Cora, do you want to watch over the young'ns again?"

Cora Skinner nodded nervously.

"Good. Once we get the wagon into the trees, you gather them children up and hunker down under the wagon. That'll be about the safest place."

"Where's Buffalo?" Judith suddenly asked.

"He'll be along directly," Barlow said. A sense of urgency had gripped him, and he didn't want such distractions. "When he does, he'll help you stand guard over the children, Miss Cora. Can you and Miss Judith shoot, Miss Hope?"

"When we have to," Hope answered. "We ain't the best shots, but we can do some damage."

"Who's the better shot between you?"

"I am," Judith said firmly.

"Good. You go get your weapons, powder and shot and all while me and Miss Hope get the wagon to cover. When them Injins show up, I want you to stand by in reserve, rifle or pistol ready, understand?"

Judith nodded firmly, though her fright was evident in her eyes.

"Miss Hope, you do the reloadin'."

"I can do that," Hope said. She moved up to the oxen and got them going. In minutes the wagon was in the foliage. Trees and brush formed a thin barrier, but it was the best they were going to find at such short notice.

Barlow dismounted and pulled his two pistols out of the saddle holster. He tied Beelzebub to a tree and took a position near the wagon. He worried that the Indians would be able to sneak up on them through the woods, but he thought they would take the easy way at first— attacking from the trail, such as it was.

They waited, quiet themselves, though little Elizabeth occasionally made some noise, and the buzzing of insects was thick and annoying. Buffalo loped up just after the group had set its defenses. His tongue lolled out, but he seemed none the worse for his run.

Ever thoughtful and practical, Hope poured some water from a barrel into a tin bowl and set it near a wagon wheel for the dog, who spent the next several minutes noisily slurping up the liquid. Suddenly his ears picked up and he growled low in his throat while baring his fangs a little.

Barlow noticed it and nodded. "So them red devils 're comin', eh, Buffler? Well, jist let 'em. They're gonna git one hell of a surprise!"

The waiting ended shortly, when Barlow eased his rifle up over the packs of his mules and fired.

The women were startled by the sudden gunfire, since none of them had seen anything out of the ordinary. But a grunt of pain and a crashing of the bushes across the trail let them know that Barlow not only had seen an Indian, but had hit him.

Then all hell broke loose, as half a dozen warriors burst out of the trees across the small trail, charging on foot toward the wagon.

Barlow grabbed up one of his pistols and fired, tossed it behind him and then grabbed the second horse pistol, which he also fired and threw behind him where Hope could grab them to reload. He noted that he had hit one Indian, who still lay on the ground, but had missed his other shot. "Fire, Judith!" he shouted as he yanked his two belt pistols out.

The young woman was scared to death, but she did as she was told, surprising herself when she actually hit a charging warrior. She fumbled with the gun a little as she tried to reload. She had seen that Hope was still busy trying to reload Barlow's guns, so she decided to do it herself. As she worked furiously, though somewhat clumsily, she noticed that the Indian she had shot had gotten up and was coming toward her. Blood covered much of his front, but she was not sure how badly he was really wounded. She almost whimpered as she tried to get her hands working properly and reload the pistol, all the while trying to keep an eye on the advancing Indian.

Suddenly two hundred and forty pounds of furry black fury darted past Judith and slammed into the warrior. Buffalo's snarls were accompanied by human shrieks as he bit and clawed chunks of flesh from the warrior, who did not live long under the ferocious assault.

Barlow fired one of his belt pistols, hitting an Indian, but another warrior was on top of him before he could use the second pistol. He ducked a tomahawk blow, dropping to the ground and rolling out of the way—and away from the wagon, under which Cora and the children cowered.

Barlow came up fast, but had lost his pistol. As he got up, he pulled out his Green River knife. The Indian stopped a few feet away, swinging his tomahawk back and forth in front of him. Barlow was not about to let the Indian—a Northern Paiute, he noted—dictate the pace or tenor of this little battle. As far as Barlow knew, there were still a few of the Paiutes running around loose, and the women were thus in danger.

He charged at the Paiute, slamming his bulk into the much smaller warrior, at the same time blocking the warrior's attempt to tomahawk him with his left forearm hitting the Indian's arm. The Paiute staggered back, until he hit one of Barlow's pack mules, which stopped him. Without letting the warrior recover his balance, Barlow stepped up and slid his knife into the Paiute's stomach and jerked it upward until he hit bone. He pulled the knife free and shoved the rapidly dying warrior away from him.

Barlow spun and saw another Paiute heading for Hope. The woman was obviously scared, but was not flustered by it. She finished reloading the pistol she held, and quickly fired it at the rushing Indian. Despite the nearness of her target, she missed him, and her face turned ashen.

Barlow raced toward the Paiute, but he was not fast enough to get to him before he backhanded Hope. The blow did not catch her fully, but it was still strong enough to knock her over. Before the warrior could get to Hope again, Barlow leaped on his back, driving the warrior to the ground, Barlow landing on top of him. Barlow reached out, grabbed the Paiute's hair and jerked his head backward, exposing his throat. Within a moment, Barlow's blade had opened him up, and blood spurted wildly from the severed carotids. Barlow let the man's head fall, and he rose, looking around, worried that more warriors were about to attack.

But the scene was quiet once again, except for the humming of the bugs, and the normal sounds of the animals.

Barlow helped Hope up. "Are you all right, ma'am?" he asked, concerned.

"I am," the woman said with as much dignity as she could muster. "It'll take more than a slap from some damned heathen to hurt me," she huffed.

Barlow smiled a little at that. "Everyone else all right?" he called out.

Judith and Cora answered in the affirmative. Buffalo bounded up to him, tail wagging, waiting to be petted. His muzzle still had traces of blood on it. Barlow knelt and scratched the huge dog's head right at the base of each ear, and Buffalo's tail wagged all the more forcefully in delight. "You done good, boy," Barlow said. "Real good." He rose. "All right, everyone, we best move on out of here and quickly. I don't think there're any more of the fractious critters around, but we can never be sure."

There was little to do, other than to retrieve dropped weapons and make sure they were all reloaded. Then they got the wagon moving again, less than five minutes after the battle had ended.

As they pulled out, Barlow decided to stick close to

the wagon for the rest of the day, just in case. Since it was late afternoon already, he didn't figure they would make much more distance at the pace they were forced to keep because of the slow-footed oxen.

Worried that the place might be a common resting spot for hunting parties and war parties, Barlow decided to bypass the copse at which he had first spotted the Northern Paiutes. They pressed on for another two miles, by which time dark was beginning to fall.

Barlow rode out a bit ahead of the poor little caravan, and was relieved when he found a fairly good place to spend the night. Since it was a bit off the faint trail, he knew he had to let the others know. If he did it himself, he would waste time that could be put to better use. He had never tried this, but he called the dog to him. If he knew how to really write, and had anything to write with, he could have tied a note to Buffalo and sent him. But he didn't so he decided to just see if Buffalo could do what was needed. "C'mere, Buffler," said. He knelt next to the big dog, so they were eye to eye. "I want you to go back to the others and bring them here, you understand me? Think you can do that, boy?" He rose. "All right, Buffler, go on, go bring them others here." He watched as the dog trotted off back down the trail.

Wondering whether the Newfoundland would actually be able to do the task, Barlow set about making the beginnings of a camp. He unsaddled Beelzebub and brushed the animal down. Then he began gathering firewood and kindling. That done, he made a fire ring and started a fire. He kept it small for now, but it was going well, and would be ready for food when the wagon rolled in. He finally sat, and stretched out his legs. He was tired from long days in the saddle, as well as the battle just a few hours earlier. He filled his pipe and lit it with a twig from the fire, and leaned back against his saddle, puffing slowly.

His worry increased as the minutes drifted by, and he soon became convinced that the women would never find him. He silently cursed himself for having sent Buf-

falo out there with no real idea of what to do. When his
pipe was done, he rose. He would have to go out and
find them himself, he decided. But as he reached for his
saddle, he heard the unmistakable protest of wagon
wheels that needed grease. He would have to do something about that soon, he figured. The sound grated on
him, though at the moment, it was the sweetest sound
he had ever heard.

He walked out toward the trail under the fast fading
daylight and watched for the wagon to come into view.
It soon did, with Buffalo happily walking a few feet in
front of the oxen. Barlow thought that if dogs could
smile, Buffalo would be doing so right now. He knelt
and patted the dog all over, gleefully praising the animal.

"That's some dog there, Mister Barlow," Judith said
as she and the others reached Barlow. "He found us and
let us know which way to go. No doubts about it." She
grinned a little.

"He's a hell of a dog, all right," Barlow agreed.
"C'mon, folks, camp's right over yonder. You can see
the light from the fire."

When they pulled into the camp, Barlow issued a few
orders. "Hope, you and Judith get the food started. Me
and Charley will see to the wagon and the oxen. Cora,
you'll see to the children?"

The women nodded, and soon the work was in pro-
gress. Before long, they were filling themselves on some
deer meat Barlow had brought in the day before, and
fine biscuits that were Hope's specialty. And not long
after, they all turned in. It had been a long, hard day,
and they were all exhausted by the rigors they had faced.

As usual, Barlow had set his otter sleeping robe a little
away from the others, and he quickly settled in, again
sleeping atop the robe. He wasn't sure how long he had
been asleep when something woke him, but he came
awake in an instant, a hand going for a pistol.

"That won't be necessary," Hope said, as she knelt
alongside Barlow.

8

BARLOW WAS STARTLED beyond words. "What the . . . ?" was all he could manage to say. He had given plenty of thought to the women in the time they had been together. And a good many of those thoughts had been carnal, though none had included Hope Skinner.

"Is there somethin' wrong, Mister Barlow?" Hope asked quietly.

"Wrong?" he said, still befuddled. "No, nothing's wrong."

"I reckon I shouldn't have come here, Mister Barlow," Hope said, sounding defeated. "It was a darn fool thing to have done." She started to push herself up.

But Barlow grabbed her arm and tugged her down so she was kneeling again. He had regained some of his composure, and hated to see her in so much turmoil. "It weren't a damn fool thing, Hope," he said, still trying to accept this. Then it dawned on him—this might not be at all what he was thinking it was. "What're you doin' here, ma'am?" he asked.

"I . . . Well, I thought . . . that it was . . ." Her face reddened, and though she knew Barlow couldn't see it in the darkness, she could sure feel it. "I'm so ashamed," she finished in a whisper.

"Ain't nothin' to be ashamed of, Hope," Barlow said. "Are you sure you want this, though?"

"Yes," she whispered, firmness in her voice.

"So soon after your husband went under?" Barlow did not like saying it, feeling that he was rubbing her nose in her grief, but it had to be done as far as he was concerned.

Hope squared her shoulders, and looked directly at the indistinct blob of Barlow's face. "Mister Skinner had many good traits, Mister Barlow. But as I said before, he also had his foolish notions. Among those was that a woman didn't need and shouldn't want some . . . intimacy. Now, many's the woman my age who might agree with that, but I ain't among 'em. Jist 'cause I'm an ol' lady don't mean I don't have a hankerin' for a man's comfortin' now and again."

Barlow was shocked, but managed not to show it. He never would have believed it from any woman—well, any white woman; Indian women were much more earthy and sensible about such things—let alone a great-grandmother like Hope Skinner. But it was a refreshing thing in its own way.

"You ain't so old, Hope," he said quietly. Though he could not really see her face now, he remembered quite well what she looked like. And, while she was old enough that he might not have paid much attention to her, he thought she retained some of her youthful beauty. And it gladdened his male ego that she would want him.

"Plenty old," Hope said, but there was a touch of humor in her voice.

"We'll just see about that," Barlow said with a grin that was seeable even in the darkness. He slid down from where he had been partly braced against his saddle, until he was lying flat on his back. "Now come on over here and straddle me."

Hope swung a leg over him and began getting ready

to settle down onto his body, when he said, "No. Up here." He indicated his face.

Hope's eyes widened. She had heard of this but had never experienced it. She had thought it was just talk, that no man would do such a thing. She was not about to argue, though. She simply squiggled forward until his hands had slid under her dress, clutched her still-firm bottom and stopped her.

Barlow was pleased that she had removed her underthings before coming here, if she even had any these days. It made things much simpler, and more enjoyable. Face covered by the swirling skirt of her dress, Barlow reached his head up in the pitch darkness, guided by scent and experience, and lightly parted the tangle of her pubic hair with his tongue, and then slithered it up and down the opening to Hope's womanhood.

Hope squirmed at the unaccustomed pleasure that shot through her. She gasped and moaned softly, without realizing at first that she was doing either.

Barlow continued to give her womanhood his full and undivided attention, using tongue, lips and even his teeth, though gently. He enjoyed the sounds of delight his actions elicited from her.

Soon Hope had to reach out and latch on to the horn of Barlow's saddle for balance. And moments later she felt an explosion start in her womanhood, a powerful blast that roared up from there and spread through her body with the strength and swiftness of a wildfire gone out of control. She shuddered with the power of it as strange sounds poured from her throat.

Barlow clung to Hope's buttocks, holding on as her passion ran its course. And as she relaxed, he took up his oral activity again, soon bringing her to another powerful climax. Then he lay his head back down, giving himself a breather.

Hope took some moments to collect herself. She had never experienced the like, and she was almost afraid to move, thinking she might fall apart. That and she wanted to savor this fascinating blissfulness buzzing through

her. She soon realized, however, that she had to move,
lest she smother the wonderful man who had given her
such pleasure. Reluctantly, she stood and stepped to one
side. "That was . . ." she said breathlessly, ". . . heavenly."

"Well, ma'am, we ain't done yet," Barlow said with
a smile, even though he knew she could not see it.

"We ain't?" Hope said, bedazzled by the delightful
feelings still racing through her blood.

"Nope."

"I ain't sure I can take any more," she said, a drawl
suddenly stretching out her words.

"The hell you can't, woman," Barlow said, his lust
evident. He unbuttoned his pants. "Now, Miss Hope,
you just tug them trousers of mine down some," he ordered quietly.

"Oh, my!" Hope said as she knelt. "Are you sure?"

"Yes'm."

She did as she was told, until Barlow's pants were
down around his knees. His manhood stood straight and
tall. "Oh, my!" Hope breathed again. "You know," she
said, "in all the years we was married, Mr. Skinner never
let me see him like this."

"Then he was a damn fool," Barlow said huskily.
"Now, straddle me and let's have us one hell of a spree."

"Yes, sir," Hope said enthusiastically. She felt fifteen
again, and ready to have a man take her for the first
time. She was almost giddy with it. She straddled him,
and began lowering herself, suddenly a little unsure of
herself, until she stopped when her womanhood brushed
the tip of his lance.

Barlow took one of Hope's hands in his and moved
it under her dress, directing it to his hardened shaft.
Wrapping her hand around his manhood, and holding it
in place gently with his own hand, he whispered, "Show
me the way."

Hope felt a surge of power and desire, and she quickly
guided him to her opening. They removed their hands,
and she slid onto his rampant manhood, shuddering with

the sheer thrill of it. She felt it filling her, and her womanly core stretching to accommodate it. It was, she decided, quite rapturous.

Slipping his hands under Hope's dress, Barlow grabbed the sides of her hips. His powerful arms lifted her and then guided her back down. It took only one more of those maneuvers before she realized what he wanted. She wanted it, too.

She began moving up and down on him then, and he let her set her own pace. It was slow at first, but within a minute, she was bouncing up and down with abandon, her breath coming quick, her moans quicker. Suddenly she screeched, the sound eerie in the otherwise quiet night.

Barlow wondered if anyone had heard, but since no one came to investigate, he decided it wasn't as loud as it had seemed.

Hope slumped down on him, breathing hard. "My lord, Mister Barlow," she panted, "you'll be the death of this ol' woman with such antics."

"You got more git up and go than most women half your age, Hope," Barlow said. He no longer thought of her as an old woman. She was just a woman with a few more wrinkles and such than many others he had encountered.

"Thank you, kind sir."

"My pleasure." He paused, then said, "Now, why don't you use some of that git up and go and let's get back to business here."

"Yes, sir!" Hope straightened up and began sliding up and down on Barlow's hardened shaft. He guided her hips with his hands for a bit, and she shifted her rhythm a little, rocking sort of back and forth instead of just up and down.

Once the movement had been established, Barlow pulled his hands out from under Hope's dress. With strong, sure fingers, he undid the buttons of her bodice, until the dress fell open, freeing her breasts. They sagged from age and years of nursing children, but Barlow didn't care. He couldn't see them much in the darkness, and to him they were soft to the touch and were capped by thick womanly nipples. He stroked Hope's breasts for a while before gently pinching her swollen nipples. Each tweak elicited a moan of pleasure from Hope.

Before long, Hope was gasping as her climax roared up on her. It exploded in her, producing great shudders of passion. Moments later, Barlow arched and bucked. He grabbed her hips outside her dress and slammed his way in and out of her womanhood, before the pleasure burst through him and he flooded her with his essence.

Hope slumped down onto Barlow, struggling to catch her breath. He was not as oxygen-deprived, but was still way behind in his breathing. Some minutes later, she pushed herself up a little, and then kissed him, forcing her tongue into his mouth.

It was, Barlow decided, not the kiss of a woman who was rapidly approaching fifty, had borne a number of children and was a great-grandmother.

"That was the most heavenly experience I've ever had, Mister Barlow," Hope said, still somewhat breathless.

"And one of mine," Barlow responded gallantly. "Now you best go on back over there by the wagon before someone misses you."

"You're right, Mister . . . Will. But I'd much rather stay right here." She rose. "Thank you, Will."

"My pleasure, Hope." Barlow lay there listening to her walk away. He heard nothing untoward after a few minutes, so he figured she got to her bedroll without arousing any suspicions. He pulled his pants back up and slid backward until his head settled against the saddle, and he closed his eyes. But sleep was not going to be his for a while. He still could not believe what had just happened. It was outlandish to even think about really. He half expected to wake up any second and realize it was all a bizarre dream.

He finally did sleep, and woke when Buffalo nuzzled him. He was groggy, and the thought of last night's occurrence popped into his mind as soon as his eyes opened. There was no getting around it, though—he knew it was true. Suddenly he chuckled to himself. "If that wasn't the damnedest thing, Buffler," he said, scratching the big dog's head.

He washed up a little and headed for the fire, wondering how he should act. He sat and silently accepted the plate of food Hope handed him. He was almost afraid to look at her, but when he did, he saw she was smiling sweetly at him. He almost smiled himself. Hope looked positively happy. He felt gladdened to know that he had brought her a little joy in what otherwise had been a drab, hard life, with the prospect of more to come.

As the simple breakfast progressed, Barlow relaxed. Cora did not appear to be aware of anything different, but Barlow noticed Judith looking at Hope with curiosity. He thought the young woman suspected something, though she said nothing. After the meal, Barlow helped the women pack up and then he rode out searching, always searching for a Shoshoni camp, a warrior named White Bear, and little girl named Anna. But this day, like so many others, was not the one when he would find his daughter, nor even a clue as to where she might be.

When he returned to the wagon that afternoon and began leading it to a site to spend the night, all the pleasures of the night before had fled from his mind. He was in a foul humor again, as he always was when worries about never finding Anna ate at him. Which they did nearly all the time.

He was relieved, too, when he was not disturbed that night or the night after. While pleasures of the flesh were always delightful, he was in no mood for companionship after more empty days of riding across the sun-baked countryside.

The days grew no cooler nor more fruitful, though several days after the attack by the Northern Paiutes, Barlow did come across a Shoshoni village. Trying to stifle the hope that had sprung into his heart, he rode toward the village. Since he did not have his pack mules with him, he had to alter the story he always used. But he had found long ago that using as much truth as possible under the circumstances was usually the best. So he told the Shoshonis that he was looking for a Northern Paiute band who had stolen two children from a traveling wagon. "You know of any bands of Northern Paiutes in these parts who might've done such a thing?" he finished.

The Shoshonis spoke among themselves for a few minutes, but then a war chief named Hawk's Bone shook his head. "We have seen no one of those people," he said in his own language, which Barlow understood enough of.

Barlow nodded. He had somehow known he would get nowhere in this village. His hope faded. Still, he had to ask about Anna. He wondered, however, how to phrase it. It seemed none of the Shoshonis he had spoken to before wanted to talk about White Bear, if he even existed. But he would not learn anything without asking. "Do you know where the village of White Bear is?" he questioned.

As soon as the words were out, the attitude of the Shoshonis changed for the worse. "I'm a friend of Casapy—the Blanket Chief," Barlow added, using the Shoshoni name for mountain man Jim Bridger, who Barlow had known only a little during his days in the mountains. But he knew enough about Bridger to know that the Shoshonis held him in high regard. "Casapy wanted me to bring a message to his old friend White Bear."

The Shoshonis' mood softened considerably, but they still insisted they did not know a warrior by that name.

Barlow spent another half-hour there, chatting idly before he rode back out of the village, the dejection weighing heavily on him, and hope fading almost to nothingness.

9

THE TEDIUM OF their slow travel expanded and grew until it seemed to fill Barlow's life. At best, they would make ten miles a day with the ponderously moving oxen, meaning it would be weeks yet before they would reach Fort Hall. Weeks wasted, as far as he was concerned, weeks that he could have spent actively searching for Anna. Not that he begrudged helping Hope and the others. He would just rather be out looking for Anna. And while he did what he could as he ranged out ahead of the onerously slow wagon, he was not free to roam as far and as fast as he would have liked. And it was all wearing on him. He had to actively fight to keep alert. It would be so easy to just nod off in the saddle most days. There was nothing much out here to keep him focused on anything.

Hope had come to him again one time a few nights after their first time together, and they had passed a pleasant hour or so, but even that was not enough to break the monotony of their travel for more than a short while. About the only thing that did occupy him more than a little was his growing friendship with Elizabeth, Judith's almost-three-year-old. The little girl reminded

Barlow so much of Anna that it was as painful to be around her as it was joyful to watch her. She was a sometimes-giggling, sometimes-serious bundle of joy and smiles and mischief.

That Elizabeth's presence was a constant, aching reminder of Anna was something Barlow decided he just had to deal with. He would rather have the toddler around, a living, breathing reminder of why he was out here.

Barlow didn't get along nearly as well with the other children—eight-year-old Rachel, eleven-year-old Charley, and five-year-old Meg. He liked them well enough, and could see that they would be fine people when they grew up, especially Charley, but there was no special connection with those others, not like there was with Elizabeth.

On occasion, Barlow would haul Elizabeth up on the big mule and take her out with him for a bit while he rode ahead. She enjoyed the little excursions as much as Barlow did, though she always fell asleep against his broad torso less than two hours after they left the wagon. When she did, he would ride back at a leisurely pace, pleased that the girl trusted him enough to rest on him, and leave her with her mother before he rode out again.

He did that one afternoon, and hadn't gone much more than a quarter-mile ahead when Buffalo began acting strangely, looking back toward where the wagon was rumbling along out of view. Barlow could not hear the wagon, which he had thought more than once was a blessing. He had one day shot a bear and that night rendered out much of the grease from the animal, which was then liberally applied to the wagon axles. It made for a much more peaceful trip, though right now Barlow wished he still could hear the ear-piercing squeak. He had not realized until now how comforting it was in some ways to be able to hear the annoying noise, for as long as it was being made, it meant the wagon was moving along without trouble.

Barlow had long ago learned to heed Buffalo's warning signs of trouble, and he was sure that's what the Newfoundland's behavior now meant—trouble. "You think we best get back to the wagon, Buffler?" he asked rhetorically. "Then let's go."

The dog turned and raced off down their back trail. Barlow kicked Beelzebub into a ground-eating trot and quickly caught up to Buffalo, and then paced the big dog. Within minutes Barlow began hearing yells from the vicinity of the wagon, and he encouraged the mule to pick up the pace a little.

Thundering toward the wagon, he pulled the mule to a stop in a cloud of dust. "What's wrong?" he asked. He saw no outright signs of attack or disaster.

"Elizabeth," Judith shrieked. "She's gone. We can't find her!"

"Damn," Barlow muttered. He dismounted and knelt next to Buffalo, who looked eager to be off. "Go find that little girl, Buffler," Barlow said quietly, calmly. "You can do it. Now go on. Find her."

The big Newfoundland bounded around the area for a bit, sniffing the air, the ground, his tail going back and forth in a rush. He seemed confused for a while, but then he let out a healthy bark and took off.

Barlow jumped back onto the mule and galloped after the dog. The others followed as quickly as they could on foot. "Good Lord Almighty," Barlow spat out. He almost brought the mule down when he jerked on the reins to stop the animal. When Beelzebub finally halted, standing, Barlow slid out of the saddle, rifle in hand. "Buffalo!" he shouted. "Back!"

He breathed a sigh of relief as the dog reluctantly stopped and backed toward him—and away from the black bear that stood protectively growling over Elizabeth's still form. Barlow dropped to one knee and brought his rifle to his shoulder and fired a moment later. A puff of dust from the bruin's coat let Barlow knew he had hit the animal, but it seemed to have no effect. Barlow stood and tossed the rifle to Cora, who was the first to arrive. "Reload it!" he ordered.

He was about to step forward when Judith roared up on the scene, screaming wildly. Barlow grabbed her and shoved her back toward her mother and grandmother. "Keep her here," he commanded before stepping forward, pulling his pistols. He fired one, then the other, dropping them after he did. The ball from each had hit the bear, but again it seemed to have little impact, other than to make the animal even angrier.

The bear suddenly reared up and Barlow bolted forward, running as hard as he could. Leaping over Elizabeth, Barlow slammed into the bruin with all the power he could muster in his two hundred fifty pound body. The crash knocked the bear over, but did not appear to hurt it any. Barlow rolled several times, and scrambled to get up. His shoulder where he had hit the bear hurt like hell, and getting up was not as easy as he thought it might be. The bear had no trouble, and growled ferociously.

Well, Barlow thought as he did get up, *at least its attention is away from Elizabeth for now.* "Go git him, Buffler," he said. "Bait that son of a bitch."

The dog charged in, nipping at the bear's heels. The bruin was fast, and kept whirling about, claws reaching for the big dog, but the Newfoundland was even quicker and always darted out of reach, only to dash back in seconds later, barking furiously all the time.

Barlow turned and ran for the mule, where he grabbed the two pistols kept in saddle holsters. He spun and charged back toward the bear. Within five feet of it, he slowed, carefully edging closer and closer. The bear reared, snarling at Buffalo. Barlow took the chance and raced in, jammed the muzzle of one pistol against the bruin's back and fired.

The blast knocked the bear onto all fours, and set its fur on fire for a moment. But it did not slow it any. It whirled with frightening speed and lashed out with its hooked claws, which tore four jagged lines down Barlow's leg from the side of his right hip to the inside part of the knee.

"Shit!" Barlow bellowed, as pain raced through his leg. But he managed to keep his feet. Tossing the empty pistol away, he jammed the other pistol into the bear's mouth and pulled the trigger.

The blast of the weapon faded into the bear's horrid growls of pain and anger. It also knocked Barlow backward and onto his buttocks. Buffalo ran up and began biting at the animal's heels again, and the bear swung around, its speed greatly diminished. As Barlow rose, he could see the gaping hole in the back of the bear's neck. The .54-caliber ball did a lot of damage at such close quarters. But the bear was not out of it yet.

Gravely wounded now, the bear wanted to get away from there, so Barlow called to Buffalo to leave the beast alone. Buffalo backed away, still snarling, his blood-coated fangs exposed. The bear moved slowly off, with Buffalo urging it on, staying just out of reach, but close enough to dart in and nip at the bear if need be.

With a heavy heart, Barlow turned and walked toward Elizabeth's limp form. He knelt beside her, and realized with a shock that she was still alive. "I'll be damned," he muttered, scratching a temple with the muzzle of the pistol he still clutched in his hand.

Elizabeth opened her eyes and smiled widely at Barlow. "Where's the big doggie?" she asked.

"Buffler?" Barlow questioned. "He's right on yonder there, making sure . . ."

"No, the other one. The rea-l-l-l-l-y big doggie."

Barlow hugged Elizabeth, smiling. "That was no doggie, little one," he said in relief. "That was a bear."

"A griddly bear?" Elizabeth asked, wide-eyed.

"No, dear, a black bear. And he was ready to make you his supper."

"He was a nice bear," Elizabeth insisted. "When I saw him, I wanted to play with him. So I followed him, but I fell asleep before we could play." She giggled, though she still looked somewhat sad.

"And you just woke up now?" Barlow was incredulous. He supposed it was true. There were no marks on

the girl that he could see. He supposed that she had
followed the bear, but then curled up and went to sleep.
The bear must've have caught her scent and came to
investigate. It was only luck—and Buffalo's keen sense
of danger, even from so far away, that had saved her.
They had arrived before the bear could harm Elizabeth
simply by pawing at her, though the bear figured that
this potential meal was his, and was planning to fight to
keep it.

"Yes. Did you send the big doggie—the *bear*—
away?"

"Yep." Barlow stood, lifting the girl into his arms as
he did. "He really wasn't a very nice bear. And Buffler
is off over there makin' sure that bear doesn't come back
here and bother you anymore."

Elizabeth looked over Barlow's shoulder and could
see the bruin still lumbering away with Buffalo herding
him. "Bye-bye, bear!" Elizabeth said gaily, waving.

Barlow shook his head as he carried the little girl back
to the others and deposited her in her mother's arms.

"Are you going out there to finish off that hideous
creature?" Cora asked.

"Nope," Barlow said. "Ain't no reason to. With all
the damage was done to him, he won't live long. So no
need for me to waste my time." He almost grinned a
little. "That is, unless you have a hankerin' for bear
meat. It's a bit on a greasy side for this ol' chil', but it
don't taste too bad."

"No, thank you," Cora said stiffly. She handed him
his rifle back, turned on her heel and walked off.

"She always that cold?" Barlow asked. He had been
meaning to question the others on it all along, but had
never seen a good opportunity.

Hope nodded. "I told my George not to go and marry
her, but he wouldn't listen to me. Now he's stuck with
a sour woman who don't do him credit."

"Well, I can live with her being that way—now that
I know it ain't me has her feathers ruffled." Barlow
turned and then whistled loudly.

Out across the meadow, Buffalo stopped harassing the bear and slowed to a stop. The big dog looked back at Barlow, who made a big looping arc with his arm. Buffalo's ears flattened and he raced toward Barlow, stopping, more or less, in a bouncing, leaping, huge bundle of furry excitement.

"You done good, boy," Barlow said, pulling a piece of jerky from his possibles bag and tossing it to the dog, who caught it in midair and chomped it a few times before swallowing it almost whole.

Everyone headed back toward the wagon, where eleven-year-old Charley was solemnly keeping watch over Rachel and Meg. He was relieved to see everyone, and especially happy that his niece had been found and was all right. Within minutes, the procession was making its ponderous way along.

Barlow rode up to Judith, who was still carrying Elizabeth, not wanting to let the girl go. Judith stopped and Barlow dismounted. "Now, you listen to me, little one," Barlow said to Elizabeth. "You don't ever go wanderin' off from here again. You had your ma scared half to death. You hear me?"

"Yessir, Mister Barlow," Elizabeth said somberly, her little face fixed in seriousness.

"That's my girl," Barlow said. He tousled the child's hair before mounting the mule again. "It's gettin' late," he announced. "I'll find us a place to stay the night soon." He rode out, Buffalo trotting alongside.

Being in the mountains now, with plenty of pine forests and aspens, decent camping spots were not hard to find. Barlow still took some time about choosing a spot, however, after he realized that it was not quite as late in the day as he had first supposed. As slow as they were traveling, every mile they could make today was one mile less to go another day. Finally, judging from the sunlight left, he found a place, and made some preliminary preparations, such as gathering some firewood and building a fire ring. As he headed back toward the wagon, he shot a deer. He was in the midst of gutting and butchering it when the wagon lurched into view. He quickly finished his work, loaded some deer meat wrapped in the animal's hide onto the wagon and then led the others to the site he had chosen.

By now, they were all used to the routine. Barlow and Charley would tend to the animals while the women and girls would set up the camp and began preparing food. The smaller ones would drag in more firewood and clean away the rocks from where they would sleep. Judith, the youngest and strongest woman, would make sure there was water if they were camped near a stream. Hope ran the show, dishing out orders in sharp, but still loving tones. No one objected, though, since she did at least as much work as anyone.

Happy to have Elizabeth back safely, the women outdid themselves in cooking that night, deciding to make it something of a celebration. Cora had found some turnips and added those to the deer meat. Hope made biscuits, sparingly using their fast-dwindling supply of flour. A little chicory was added to the pot of coffee to give it a bit more flavor. And for afterward, there was a cherry cobbler, made of desiccated cherries the women had hauled along for the whole trip. Hope had decided now was the time to bring them forth.

It was a festive little supper for the small group. They talked of non-important matters, avoiding chat of their losses for this one night, thankful that they were alive and that they had made it this far. The women felt safer with Barlow along, and, while they would not admit it aloud, each had hopes that the big block of former mountain man would help them get where they were going. And they thought that since it had been so fortuitous that he had come along, they also hoped that it was a sign that they would eventually get their captive children back.

Since there was plenty of meat, Barlow ate like he did back in his mountain days—prodigiously, consuming startling amounts of meat. It always shocked the women to see him do so, not so much that he seemed piggish, but that he was capable of such feats. He had caught them staring at him once and when he questioned why, he responded to them by laughing and saying, "All the ol' mountain boys're the same when it comes to feedin' that way. You always take your fill for you never know when you'll be fillin' your meatbag again."

So he was full and content when he finally leaned back against a log and tamped tobacco into his pipe and lit it. He felt ever better two hours later when he heard someone approaching him in the night. He smiled.

10

BARLOW WAS IN for another surprise. He sat up on his otter robe when Judith called his name. "I'm awake," he said cautiously, wondering if she were here for the reason he hoped she was. He had lusted after Judith Dockery since he had first seen her lithe figure. Since then, he had become more desirous of having her, because she was a fine woman as well as a beautiful one. A man could do a lot worse than Judith Dockery for a wife, was he of a mind for such doin's, which he wasn't. At least not yet. Maybe after he found Anna, he would consider such a thing, but not now.

Judith came up and squatted next to Barlow. "You mind some company, Mister Barlow?" she asked. Her voice had edges of nervousness, but there was lust there, too.

"Not at all, Miss Judith." He licked his lips. "You have somethin' to say? Somethin' you need to ask, maybe?"

"Well, both, I reckon. I wanted to thank you for helpin' us all this time. I know it must be very difficult stayin' with us when you'd rather be out lookin' for your little girl."

"Well, a man's gotta do what he's called on to do, Miss Judith," Barlow said seriously. The pain in his heart awoke a little bit, but he pushed it down. He was getting good at doing that, maybe too good, he sometimes thought.

"Well, it's still a darn fine thing, Mister Barlow. We would've been dead for sure by now if you hadn't come along when you did. Or captured like my little Sam Junior and poor Georgie." She fought back a sob.

"Like I said, ma'am," Barlow reiterated, "sometimes a man gets called on to do certain things. He might not always want to do them right at that time, but if he's any kind of real man, he's got to put aside his own feelin's and see to whatever it is has been set forth for him."

Judith nodded. With a few tears on her cheeks, Barlow thought she looked absolutely beautiful in the light from the full moon and many stars.

"I also wanted to thank you for savin' my Elizabeth today." She shuddered at the thought of what could have happened if Barlow hadn't returned when he did.

"My pleasure, ma'am," Barlow said with a small smile. "But you need to thank Buffler there as much as me. That ol' dog is somethin' now, or I wouldn't say so. He knew—he just *knew*—somethin' was amiss here, and wouldn't let me go on without we checked it first."

"He is some dog, Mister Barlow," Judith said. "And, well, I'd like to thank him, too, but I can't say as he'd like what I had in mind, was I to try to show him my thanks the way I was fixin' to show you." Her voice was still edgy, but had gotten bolder, too.

"And how is that, Miss Judith?" Barlow asked, mouth suddenly gone dry.

"I only know one way a woman can truly show thanks to a good man," Judith said brazenly. "And I have a deep hankerin' to show you my thanks, Mister Barlow. If you want me to." A bit more nervousness crept into her voice.

"If I want you to, eh?" Barlow said, trying to keep

the lust out of his own voice. "I've had trouble thinkin' of anythin' else since I been with you all."

"Why didn't you never say anything?" Judith asked, somewhat surprised. She had never known he felt that way, though she had often wished he would want her that way. She had been powerfully attracted to him right from the start.

"Never felt it was my place, ma'am," Barlow said evenly. "You was a married woman, even if that damn fool of a husband went off and left you for another." He shook his head in amazement. "I can't believe any man who could call himself a man would be so damned stupid."

"Thank you, Mister Barlow." She paused. "I was bothered more than a mite when it first happened, of course, but then I realized soon after that I was better off without that horrid man. To tell the truth, he weren't much of a man anyway."

"It's his loss, Miss Judith. Anyway, I didn't know none of that. So I didn't think it my place to say somethin' of such an intimate nature to you."

Judith smiled. "Well, I wish you would've, Mister Barlow. We've wasted a good bit of time. But that's all behind us now. We got some makin' up of missed chances to do."

"That shines with this ol' chil'," Barlow said fervently.

Judith rose, undid some buttons and a moment later let her simple cloth dress slide off her to the ground. The moonlight splayed across her ripe young body, highlighting the firm, big-nippled breasts, the gentle swell of belly with the deep-set navel, and leaving in shadow the dark, tangled mass of hair covering her womanhood.

"My God, woman, if you ain't somethin' to look at," Barlow said honestly, almost in wonder.

"Thank you, Mister Barlow," Judith said, almost seeming to blush. "But I don't figure me standin' here

buck nekkid is gonna do us much good with you all
swathed in your clothes like you are."

Barlow grinned broadly. "I reckon you're right about
that, woman." He stood and swiftly shucked his clothes
until he was as naked as she was. He stepped up to her
and pulled her into his arms. His manhood started to rise
at just the touch of her flesh against his. He responded
even more strongly when he kissed her hard, long and
deep.

Judith almost melted when she saw Barlow nude, and
then when he gathered her in, she was in heaven. Her
knees did give way a bit when he kissed her, his tongue
seeking hers in the hot recesses of her mouth. But she
recovered and responded willingly, avidly devouring
him.

Barlow pulled back a bit and then bent and scooped
her up. He knelt and lay her on the otter skin sleeping
robe. Still at her side, he leaned over her, bracing himself
on his hands, and kissed her long and deep again. She
wrapped her hands around the back of his neck, holding
his mouth tightly to hers. He pulled back again and left
a trail of hot, moist kisses down her chin, her throat and
the valley between her breasts to her deep navel. He
retraced his path until he reached her breasts. He suckled
at one while he hand caressed the other. After some
minutes of that, he switched and gave the other breast
the same careful attention.

By now Judith was wriggling steadily, moaning low
in her throat, and clawing at his back with ragged fin-
gernails.

Barlow continued kissing her breasts and sucking at
her nipples, going from one to the other. A hand slid
down her body until it cupped her damp womanhood.
His thick middle finger pushed its way through the mat
of wet hair until it found the soft, spongy lips underneath. The finger lanced strongly and surely into her
inner being, bringing forth a deep, longing moan. While
the finger wriggled inside her, Barlow's thumb made
small, insistent circles on her love bud.

Judith wrapped her fingers in Barlow's long, unruly hair and tugged this way and that as her climax began to build, growing stronger by the moment. It burst inside her, sending a shockwave of intensity roaring through her body. She quivered and shook from the power of it, and breathed in short, choppy gasps.

Barlow lifted his head and grinned at her. She grinned back, and brushed the back of a hand across the sheen of sweat on her forehead.

Barlow started his hand movements on and in her vulva again, and kissed her deeply. It reignited the passion in Judith right away, and she moaned joyfully. It grew and grew, rising like the sun on a hot summer's day, steadily heading upward, bringing with it tremendous heat and brightness.

Her second climax hit her like a cannon blast, and she was left gasping from its power. "No more," she panted, not really meaning it, but a little worried that she would not be able to survive another burst as powerful as this one had been.

"Yes, more," Barlow said, before smashing his lips on hers again and returning to his hand movements. He slipped another finger inside her and began a scissorslike action with the two digits, while continuing to tend carefully to her love bud with this thumb.

"Yes, more!" Judith agreed as the flames lit her womanly desire again, sparking a hunger for more of him, more of this wonderful feeling. She had never felt such things before. Sam Dockery had been like most men that she had heard about—no better than a perfunctory lovemaker. In the almost four years she had been married she had not had as much rapture as she had received from Will Barlow in just the past twenty minutes. "Yes, more, more!" she repeated. "Lots more!"

Her words gave way to more moans and gasps as she was overcome with the intensity of the feelings that flooded through her. Unconsciously, her back arched, and she thrust her pelvis up to meet Barlow's vigorous movements, as if she were trying to engulf his whole hand.

He smiled as he worked his mouth down to her breasts again and began licking and sucking on the succulent, crimson-tipped globes. Judith lifted her head and nuzzled Barlow's neck. When the next climax sent Judith over the edge moments later, she screamed into Barlow's hair and neck, hoping somewhere in the back of her mind that her sound was muffled enough to not arouse the others. It would not do to have her mother find her in such a way. Her grandmother, she thought, would not say anything. Might even be proud of her. Besides, she had her suspicions about the older woman.

As the shudders of her latest climax subsided, she whispered to him, "Your turn, Will. Take me. Please."

Barlow needed no further encouragement. He shifted until he was between her legs, her womanhood open to him, inviting his entry. He studied her that way for a moment, enjoying what he could see of her in the shadows. He moved up on her, then guided himself to her opening, then eased into her with a slow, steady, strong pressure. The feel of her body expanding in perfect timing to accept him was almost overwhelming. It surged through his lance, powering its way through his body. It was an indescribable sensation. He pushed a little more and then more, pausing to let her accommodate him, and for him to savor the delicious sensation it produced in him.

And then he was in her all the way, and both of them treasured the feeling. Finally, Barlow eased himself almost all the way out and began thrusting in and out with sureness and power. His movements were slow at first, but quickly began increasing in speed and intensity.

Judith thrilled at the feeling of having her most intimate self invaded by this gentle but strong man. She relished it for a bit, but then she decided to try something she had never had an opportunity to try before. She began moving her hips, almost circling her buttocks, matching the rhythm of Barlow's plunge and retreat, plunge and retreat. Her movements—and his—produced an extraordinary sensation that flooded her body, making her quiver with bliss.

Barlow's thrusting shifted to an even faster pace and he seemed almost frantic. Suddenly he grunted wildly, and his torso bent backward as his passion boiled into Judith's insides. The veins on his stretched neck bulged as he bucked with the strength of his climax.

Judith was right behind him, almost snorting as she felt his essence bathe her innermost parts. The physical sensation combined with the emotional pleasure to produce a powerful release. She shoved the back of her hand into her mouth to prevent her screams of delight from bursting forth and waking everyone else in the camp.

Barlow flopped to Judith's side and lay on his back, trying to catch his breath. She slipped into the crook where his arm and shoulder met, resting her head there, and placing a hand on his massive chest. She, too, was having trouble catching up with her breathing.

Finally, Judith pushed up onto an elbow and looked at Barlow's big, broad face. She smiled, and was pleased to see that it was returned. "Did I thank you well enough, Mister Barlow?" she asked coyly.

"Yes, ma'am," Barlow said with quiet enthusiasm. "More than well enough. Best thankin' I ever got."

"I'm glad." She paused, tracing lines across his face with a forefinger. "You know, Mr. Barlow, ain't no man ever did what you done to me. And ain't no man ever made me feel the way you made me feel tonight."

"Was my pleasure, Judith," Barlow said softly.

"I just wanted you to know how grateful I am for you takin' care of my needs the way you done."

"You're grateful?" Barlow questioned with a great big grin. "That means you need to thank me agin, don' it?" His grin grew even more.

"You want more thankin'?" Judith asked, eyes wide. After Sam had made love to her, he wanted nothing more to do with her. Now here this man was asking her for more of the most tender intimacies with her.

"You're damn right I do," Barlow said fervently. "That bother you?"

"No, sir," Judith responded firmly. "I just didn't know if you might've been funnin' me or somethin'. Mister Dockery never wanted to . . . well . . ."

"Listen to me, Judith," Barlow said seriously, cupping her chin in a big paw, "I don't fun about such things. And you already know my opinion of your . . . husband. The man ain't got the sense God give a rock."

Judith smiled. "I believe you. Thank you."

"My pleasure." Barlow smiled back.

"You really want more thankin'?" she asked with a giggle.

"Like I said, damn right I do. I jist ain't up to it at the moment, but you give me a bit of rest here, and I'll take to ravishin' you good and proper before you know it."

"I can wait," Judith said happily as she snuggled against him again.

An hour later, Barlow made good on his promise. He tasted her whole body, a little at a time, savoring every delicious morsel. And his hands explored every nook and cranny, teasing, touching, stimulating her. She lost count of the small climaxes she experienced. She just enjoyed every second, every tender caress, every lick, suck, kiss and nip. She gave back to him when he would allow it, and when she was able. Frequently, though, she was in the throes of excitement and could not get her brain to work enough to do much for him. He didn't seem to mind.

Judith thought it most extraordinary when he finally rolled over onto his back and told her to straddle him. She did so willingly, not needing to be told what to do once she got there. She impaled herself on his rigid shaft and bounced with abandon on top of him, reveling in the feel of his manhood stretching and filling her. And when he reached his peak seconds after she did, she felt light-headed with the explosiveness of her climax. She thought for a moment that she would faint from it. Instead she just flopped forward atop Barlow and lay there, almost crying at the beauty of it all.

Before long, however, she had caught her breath, and knew she had to leave him. She kissed him longingly and lingeringly, then reluctantly pulled on her simple dress and headed back to the wagon, feeling so vibrant that she might not ever need to sleep again. Or care about it.

11

THERE WERE TIMES when Barlow had been sure he would never see the day, but Fort Hall finally came into view. They plodded slowly on, Barlow chafing all the more. Now that the place was in sight, Barlow just wanted to gallop there and get away from this damn wagon. But he stayed behind, riding alongside the ponderous conveyance.

Three weeks to the day had passed since he and Buffalo had rescued little Elizabeth from the bear. Judith had shown up almost every night during that time, and the two of them had made love with wild abandon. When she didn't arrive one night, Barlow was a little put out. Over breakfast the next morning, he questioned her with raised eyebrows.

"Talk later," she whispered before hurrying away.

He was saddling Beelzebub when Judith sidled up. "I'm sorry, Mister Barlow," she said quietly, her voice revealing that her apology was sincere. "I couldn't come to you last night because . . ." She hung her head in embarrassment. "Well, I'm not clean . . . I . . ."

"Not clean?" Barlow queried, not understanding.

"Yes, you know . . . When a woman . . ."

"Oh." He paused. "Oh!" He suddenly realized what she was saying. "I understand, Judith," he added. "I was thinkin' maybe I'd done somethin' that didn't sit well with you and I was tryin' to figure out what it was I done."

"You've done nothing wrong, Mister Barlow. Not at all." She stopped and looked around, wondering if she should continue. She decided to do so. "I'll come back to you as soon as I'm . . . not unclean again. If you still want me to, that is." She sucked in a breath and held it.

"You might've heard this before, Miss Judith," Barlow said with a smile tugging at the corners of his mouth. "But you're damn right I do." He grinned.

Judith's breath rushed out in relief. She had been deathly afraid that he would reject her out of hand. She glanced around, making sure no one was looking, quickly kissed him and then ran off.

Barlow stood there for a moment, watching her, and rubbing the stubbled cheek where she had just bussed him. She was, he decided, a hell of a woman, and he would love to have her as his permanently, but that was out of the question for anytime in the foreseeable future. First he had to find Anna. Only then could he think about another mate.

In the interim, Hope had returned. Though nothing was said, Barlow suspected that she and her granddaughter either knew about each other's involvement with him, or strongly suspected it.

Five nights later, Judith was back in his "bed" with him, and they were enjoying plenty of carnal pleasures, most of which she had never even conceived of. But she enjoyed them all, and gleefully, happily, willingly took part with every bit of enthusiasm she had in her.

Judith's heart fell, though, when they spotted Fort Hall a few days after that. Once they were at the fort, she knew, there would be no more trysts with Barlow. He would be gone, off on the hunt for his daughter, and she would be caught up in whatever could be done to try to find her own son, Sam Junior, and Cora's son,

Georgie. She was certain she would never see Barlow again once they rode into the fort.

They came toward the post from the southeast, so they did not pass the tipi brothel that Old Man Verhoeven ran. Barlow decided he would have to stop by later and see that Verhoeven and his son were treating Beatrix right. Besides, he might have need of her services. He had become used to having Judith every night lately, and that was about to end now that they had arrived at the fort.

While they were still a quarter of a mile away, a small contingent of men rode out from the fort and greeted them. Barlow did not really know any of the men in the welcoming party, but one introduced himself as Robert Davison, a clerk for the Hudson's Bay Company. "And who might you be?" he asked politely.

Barlow introduced himself, and then began naming the women, starting with Hope. That was as far as he got before Davison asked, "Are you related to George Skinner?"

"I am," Hope said eagerly. "He's my son. Cora," she added, pointing, "is his wife. Is George here?"

"Aye, mum, that he is," Davison said. "He arrived a few days ago and has been trying to put together a force to find you."

"Ah, good," Hope said, smiling broadly. "Is he still here?"

"Aye, mum. He's been recovering from his ordeal. I understand you were attacked? By Shoshonis?"

"Yes," Hope said. "Well, we were attacked. We thought it was by Shoshonis, but Mister Barlow assured us they were not."

"And just what do you know about this affair, Mister Barlow?" Davison asked, looking at Barlow.

"Only that from what these people told me, it weren't Shoshonis," Barlow said tightly. He didn't care for Davison's manner. "From what they described to me, I figure it was Northern Paiutes. I also think that because the

Shoshonis ain't ever been disposed to take white captives."

"Captives?" Davison asked, surprised.

"Mr. Skinner never said anything?" Hope asked.

"No, mum. Not about captives."

"Those savages took two from us—Judith's son, Sam Junior, and Cora's son, Georgie," Hope said, fighting back some anger. "You're sure my son never mentioned them?"

"I am, mum." Davison looked at Barlow. "So you think it was Northern Paiutes because the Shoshonis don't take captives?"

Barlow nodded.

"From what I hear, the Shoshonis have your daughter captive."

Barlow sat silent for a moment, letting his anger dwindle. "That's true," he finally said. "But they didn't take her."

Davison stared at him for a moment before dropping his eyes under the heat of Barlow's glare. "Well, let's get these people to the post," he finally said. He turned his horse and began riding back. The other men followed, slowly, as each took some time to stare openly at Judith mostly, but Cora, too.

Davison led the wagon to a place outside the fort—a pleasant glade amongst a well-wooded area. It was right near the Snake River. The old wagon creaked to a halt, finally, and the women began setting up their camp. Barlow wanted to just head into the fort and be done with the wagon, but he felt an obligation to help the women and children one last time. So he pitched in, and when things were done, he rode on over into the post.

He went straight to the blacksmith's shop and left Beelzebub and the two pack mules to be looked over. They had been pretty hard used and needed some extra care. Then he went over to the shed that served as a dining room. It was no better this time than it had been the last time he had been here. The repulsive cook slapped some bowls of foul-looking, fetid slop in front of him. Barlow was just about to dig in to the repugnant meal when he decided he'd rather die first. He rose and left, Buffalo walking at his side. He borrowed a horse from the blacksmith and rode to the women's camp. He stopped and dismounted. Sort of scuffing the toe of his moccasins in the dirt, he asked, "Would you ladies mind if I was to set to supper with you?"

"Not at all, Mister Barlow!" Hope said with a big smile. "We'd be honored to have you."

Out of the corner of his eye, Barlow could see Judith grinning widely. "Thank you, ma'am." He grinned a little himself. "I couldn't face eatin' whatever swill that damn fool at the fort was dishin' up."

"Well, we have some of that antelope left from yesterday, and some taters. And some other things. I think you'll be happier with that than you would with anything you'd get in the fort."

"That's a fact, ma'am." Barlow walked off, tugging the borrowed horse after him, and tied the animal to a tree. Then he went and took a seat on a tree stump near the fire. It was almost as if nothing had changed from the previous several weeks.

He was still sitting there, playing with Elizabeth, when a medium-size man of average build rode into the little camp. He dismounted, giving Barlow a sour glance. He tossed the reins of his horse toward Charley. "Take care of my horse, boy," he commanded. He surveyed the camp. His arrogance seemed to dissipate as Cora came up to him and smiled.

"Welcome back, George," she said.

"It's good to see you, Cora."

"Supper's almost ready. Go sit by Mister Barlow."

"Who's he?" George asked, looking sourly at Barlow again.

"He's the man who led us to salvation out of the wilderness," Hope said. She was not pleased with the way her son had turned out, and her disappointment showed.

Skinner nodded, displeased with this turn of events. He sat on another stump across the fire from Barlow. "I hear you helped my family get here to safety," he said, his discontent evident in his voice.

Barlow didn't like Skinner's tone nor his demeanor. "I only did what was needed. What someone else should have done." He looked pointedly at Skinner, while still bouncing Elizabeth on one knee. The girl was giggling wildly.

"Are you sayin' I let my family down?" Skinner demanded, growing angry.

"That's enough of that for now," Hope said firmly. "Supper's ready and we should put aside this harsh talk, at least while we're feedin'."

"Yes'm," Barlow said. He set Elizabeth down. "Go on and help your mama, little one," He smiled watching the girl toddle off.

The meal was something of a painful affair, with everyone mostly quiet, focusing on their food and avoiding conversation. Barlow controlled himself, not putting away his usual enormous amounts of food. And soon he sat back, lighting his pipe.

Skinner finished soon after. As he tossed his plate to the dirt, he looked at Barlow and said, "Now, sir, did you mean to infer that I left my family in trouble?"

"What do you think, ol' hoss?" Barlow countered. "You left your women and young'ns out there on their own, after just bein' attacked by red devils, to fend for themselves, while you mosey along till you reach this fort and then loll about here, makin' little effort to go out and bring 'em to safety."

"But that ain't the way . . ."

"And even worse, hoss, you didn't even have the stones to tell the folks here at the fort that two of the young'ns was took by them damn savages."

"I resent your implications, Mister," Skinner said, seething.

Barlow shrugged. "You hadn't left these women and children out there to fend for themselves, boy, you wouldn't have to set here and hear such things."

"Damn you, boy! Damn you!" Skinner snapped. "You

don't know what it was like out there. You . . ."

"You hush up, boy," Hope said angrily. "I told you not to go and leave us to make our own way out there, but you wouldn't listen. You rode on out, endangering yourself as well as all the rest of us. We would have perished out there in that desert or wilderness, if the Good Lord hadn't sent Mister Barlow to us."

"Don't start in on me, Ma," Skinner protested.

"I said hush, boy. I ain't done. I was plannin' to ask you this soon's I could, and this seems as good a time as any. Why didn't you tell the folks here at the fort about Sam Junior and Georgie being took by those savages?"

"I was fixin' to, ma. I just hadn't had the right . . ."

"How could you not tell them right off?" Hope demanded, thoroughly disgusted with her son. "There weren't ever gonna be a better time than that."

"But, Ma . . ."

"Don't you 'but' me, boy," Hope said, her anger bubbling over. "We're talking your own flesh and blood here. Your namesake son!"

"I don't figure you know all . . ."

"I'd quit while I still had some dignity left, boy, was I you," Barlow said.

"Keep the hell out of my family business, you no-account son of a bitch," Skinner spit.

Barlow bolted up from his seat, leaped over the fire, grabbed Skinner's shirt in both hands and hauled him up. "Don't nobody talk to me in such a way, hoss," Barlow said quietly, though his rage was evident in his eyes. "And you ought to be man enough to stand up to your mama and tell her you took the coward's way out. And then you ought to plead for her forgiveness. She's a good woman, and undeservin' of havin' a skunk like you for a son." Barlow slammed Skinner back down on his seat and turned to head back to his own.

"Damn you!" Skinner roared as he charged toward Barlow, plowing into the former mountain man's back, and grabbing him around the chest, barely. He drove

Barlow a few steps forward, but not down to his knees as he had expected to do.

Barlow finally got his feet planted solid, and stopped moving. He took one of Skinner's thumbs in a huge hand and began twisting it. Behind him, Skinner hissed in pain, and unlaced his hands. He stumbled around to the side under the unrelenting pressure on his thumb.

When Barlow had Skinner in front of him, he punched the man square in the face, somewhat pleased at the sound of Skinner's nose crunching. He didn't use all his strength, but the blow was enough to let Skinner know what he was in store for if he continued trying to cause trouble.

Skinner reeled under the punch, but did not fall.

"Now, hoss, I reckon you ought to go back to that fort as soon as you're able and tell them boys the whole tale. I don't reckon they'll be willin' to help you go find them children of yours, but you ought to at least ask." He released Skinner's thumb. "And I reckon you should try actin' like a man from here on out, boy."

Barlow turned and headed toward the borrowed horse. He got a few feet, then stopped and turned. "And next time you come agin me, boy, you best be prepared to meet your Maker. I ain't the kind to abide people attackin' me and lettin' 'em walk away from it."

He climbed onto the horse. Looking at Hope, he said, "I'm obliged for the supper, ma'am. And I'm sorry about the ruckus." A smiled tugged at his lips. "But if you need my help for anything, you come see me."

"I'll do that, Mister Barlow," Hope said, torn between the seriousness of the situation and the memories she had of this hard young man making love to her in the darkness. "But I think my George will behave himself from here on, won't you Georgie?"

Skinner refused to answer; he just stood there, dazed, rubbing his abused thumb.

"I expect you're right, Miss Hope," Barlow said. "But you keep what I said to mind. Night, ma'am. Ladies."

He grinned. "Night, little one," he added, waving at Elizabeth, who giggled and waved her tiny hand back at him. With a last glare of warning at Skinner, Barlow turned the horse and rode out of the camp.

12

BARLOW WAS UP before first light the next morning. Girding himself, he went to the dining room and forced down the swill he was served by the sullen cook. From there he went to the blacksmith shop, where he began loading his supplies—what was left of them—on his two pack mules. As he did so, the stomach eruptions that resulted in foul emanations from mouth and buttocks made him regret having partaken of breakfast in this place. He would have done better to just gnawed on some jerky while he rode. But it was too late for that now. He would just have to live with the odious recollection of the loathsome meal.

With the mules loaded, Barlow saddled Beelzebub and mounted up. Without regret, he rode out of the fort. He had spoken to the factor the night before after returning from the women's camp, and once more had asked for help in finding Anna.

As he had before, factor Finan McTavish turned Barlow down. "I canna do anything for ye, Mr. Barlow," McTavish said, shrugging as if helpless. "Even if I knew where to find this White Bear you think has the lass, I canna spare the men to help ye."

Barlow nodded. He had been sure he would get such a response, but had to give McTavish a chance to relent and be of some use. "And how about the Skinners and all?" he asked. "You aim to send them off without helpin' to find their young'ns, too?"

"Mr. Skinner nae said anythin' aboot missin' lads or lasses, Mr. Barlow," McTavish said, his tone chiding.

"That's because Mr. Skinner is a cowardly sack of prairie dog shit," Barlow snapped. "But they lost two young'ns to the savages."

"Well, I dunna know anythin' aboot any of that, Mr. Barlow," McTavish said, his manner indicating an apology that was not in evidence in his voice. "But if they were to come to me and ask for help, I'd have to take their request under consideration."

"Anybody ever tell you that you're a goddamn contemptible ol' bastard?" Barlow snapped, disgusted with McTavish and just about everyone connected with Fort Hall.

"I think our business is concluded, Mr. Barlow," McTavish said stiffly. "You will be leaving the fort soon, aye?"

"First thing tomorrow. 'Less'n somethin' turns up to keep me here, which ain't goddamn likely."

"I wish you well in your search for your daughter, Mr. Barlow," McTavish said with a complete lack of sincerity.

Barlow nodded and walked out, still considering the possibility of siccing Buffalo on the insufferable fort factor. He decided that doing such a thing would endanger his dog because McTavish was almost certainly composed of tainted meat.

So, he had no regrets when he rode out the next morning, the big Newfoundland trotting happily alongside. He rode silently past the quiet camp of women and children, pausing only long enough to make sure that everything seemed fine. He also rode past Verhoeven's tipi brothel. In the light just edging into the sky, Barlow could see Beatrix's lodge. Nothing seemed amiss, and he hoped the woman was all right. He considered stopping and making sure she was well, but he decided he did not want to know if there was a chance she was not. That would only delay him more while he meted out an appropriate punishment to Old Man Verhoeven and his son, Hans. He had wasted enough time already. Summer was on the wane, and he was no closer, really, to finding Anna than he had been when he first arrived at Fort Hall.

He turned southwest, and gradually picked up the pace. He suddenly felt a renewed sense of urgency. Still, he had nothing to do for a while but think, at least while he was within a day's ride of the fort. Beyond that, he would have to pay more attention to the countryside and what it might tell him, but for now, he was alone with his thoughts. And he began to wonder just why no one seemed to have heard of White Bear—or of a white captive. He figured that McTavish's hunters, trappers and traders should know the Shoshoni, since they traded so heavily with that tribe. And he figured that they should have heard of White Bear, and certainly that there was a young white girl captive in a village somewhere. That they had not seemed mighty odd to Barlow. Which led him to the belief that perhaps they were lying about it. But that made no more sense than not having heard of the Shoshoni warrior he sought.

It was a mystery that kept Barlow deeply puzzled for some time. Not that solving the mystery meant much to him. He cared not a whit for McTavish's reasoning, other than it made finding Anna more difficult. Still, it gnawed at him that McTavish's obstinacy made his search more troublesome.

Riding as long as he could every day, and stopping only when necessary, Barlow covered in a few days the distance it had taken the wagon a few weeks to make. He had decided shortly after leaving the fort that he would try to track down the band that was responsible for the Northern Paiute war party with which he and the women had fought. There was a chance that the Paiutes

might know something about White Bear and the Shoshonis, and be willing to talk. While the Northern Paiutes and the Shoshonis were not really enemies, there
was often no love lost between the two tribes. That
might help the Paiutes open up.

He stopped at the site where the fight had taken place.
There was little sign left of the battle save for some
bones scattered about. Barlow thought that a bit strange
at first, but he quickly concluded that no one had found
the slain warriors. The bears, wolves and coyotes, as
well as the vultures, had feasted on the corpses, strewing
the bones hither and yon in the doing. The Indian ponies
would have drifted off, and were either living with some
herd of wild horses somewhere, or had been caught by
other Indians. The fact that it looked like no one had
been here since the fight worked in Barlow's favor. He
had worried some that this particular band of Northern
Paiutes might have come along and found their comrades, and so know who had defeated the warriors, thus
making it mighty dangerous for him to try to parley with
them. But from the looks of things on the killing ground,
the dead warriors had not been found, so the village
from which they came probably had no idea what happened to them. That was fine with Barlow.

There was enough sign to follow, at least for a while,
and Barlow made pretty good time for a day or so. But
since so many days had passed since he had been here
last, the signs quickly faded, until there was almost
nothing for him to track. He pushed on in the general
direction from which he thought the war party had
come.

Late in the afternoon of the fourth day after leaving
the battlefield, Barlow pulled Beelzebub to a halt. He sat
staring at the horizon, and smiled grimly. The circling
of so many turkey vultures in one spot could mean only
one thing out here—an Indian village. With increasing
hope—and dread—he pushed on, moving quickly. He
was anxious to be in the village now, hoping that his

quest would soon be at an end, though he knew that was unlikely.

As usual, several warriors galloped out to see who the approaching traveler was. They swooped around him, yipping war cries and shaking their lances and rifles at him, their painted ponies prancing.

Barlow stopped the mule and sat, affecting a bored look as he watched their antics, which were designed to see if he would frighten easily.

When it became obvious that he would not, the warriors settled down, and one said in poor English, "Why you here?"

"I want to parley with your chiefs," Barlow answered calmly.

"Why?"

"None of your goddamn business, hoss," Barlow snapped. "Now, are you gonna take me over there and let me parley with your chiefs or am I gonna have to give you a lead pill plumb center in that ugly face of yours?" He lifted his Henry rifle from where it lay across the saddle in front of him, until the butt was resting on his right thigh, and the muzzle was pointing skyward. He had had the rifle since fighting in the Black Hawk War more than a decade ago. Several years ago, he had had a gunsmith at Fort Vancouver convert it to percussion from flintlock, after considerable thought. It was easier that way, though the chance of running out of caps out in the wilderness was a vexing point.

The warrior did not look happy at being spoken to in such a way, but he had suddenly realized, too, that this big, broad white man was not someone to be trifled with, and while he might die at the hands of the warrior and his friends, he would not go under alone.

"Come," the surly warrior said, jerking his head toward the village that could be dimly seen on the horizon.

Surrounded by the small group of Paiutes, Barlow rode silently, unconcerned, toward the village. He stopped when the lead warrior told him to, though instead of waiting out in the center of the village where

he was on open display, he eased Beelzebub over toward
a thicket of brush. He dismounted and tied the mule and
the pack animals to the bushes, then loosened the saddle
so Beelzebub could breathe. The three mules began
cropping grass, oblivious to whatever was going on
around them.

Barlow took several swallows of hot water from his
canteen and then poured some water into his hat so Buffalo could drink, which he eagerly did. Barlow slapped
the hat back on, letting the small remains of water drip
down his face and the back of his neck, mingling with
the sweat but feeling cooler and more refreshing. He
pulled out two ragged strips of jerky. Squatting alongside the dog, he gave the Newfoundland one of the
slices, then tore off a piece of the other, slowly masti-
cating it, hating the toughness of it.

The warrior who had led him to the village came for
him soon after. "Come," he said, spinning and starting
to walk away. He made several steps before he realized
that Barlow was not behind him. He stopped and turned.
"You come. Now. Chiefs parley. Now. Come." He
waved his arm urgently.

Barlow calmly reached over and petted Buffalo, ig-
noring the warrior.

The Paiute stomped back up to him and said loudly,
"You come. Now. Goddammit. You come."

"You're a right pain in my ass, boy," Barlow said,
standing. "It don't shine with this ol' hoss to be spoke
to in such a manner."

The warrior stood there for some moments, digesting
that. He wasn't sure of the whole meaning of what Barlow had said, but he knew it was a poor reflection on
him. "The chiefs, they wait. You parley. Come."

"You askin' me to come along? Not tellin' me?" Barlow didn't know why he was being so obstinate right at
the moment. It simply seemed the right thing to do.

"Ask, yes," the warrior said, trying to smile. "Not tell.
Ask. Yes. Come now."

"Well, hell, why didn't you say so, boy?" Barlow countered with a sarcastic grin.

The Paiute grimaced at him and then turned and stomped off. Barlow and Buffalo followed, but at a leisurely pace, the man checking out the sights, the dog sniffing the air, hoping to find a female in heat. The warrior finally held open the flap to a big lodge. Barlow started to enter, with Buffalo eagerly waiting his turn, when the escort said, "Dog no go in."

"Piss on you, boy," Barlow said almost cheerfully. He went in, and Buffalo followed. The Paiutes inside looked a little annoyed, but Barlow didn't care. He was tired of all the nonsense. He simply wanted to ask these people if they knew where the Shoshoni named White Bear was and then be gone. He knew he would not find his Anna here. He hated all the wasteful ceremony and extreme politeness that went on in these parleys. He sat, crosslegged on the dirt floor, and Buffalo stretched out beside him.

"Welcome," one of the eight older Paiutes sitting at the fire said in a deep, resonant voice. He was obviously a chief of some stature here.

"Thankee," Barlow said edgily. He was tempted to just blurt out his question and be done with it, but he knew that would only insult his hosts, and would mean he would get no information if there was any to be had here.

"I am Two Hawks," the head man said. "We will eat, then smoke, Then we parley. Yes?"

Barlow nodded. Though the Paiute had phrased it as a question, there was no doubt that it was a statement. He waited, chafing again at the delay. It seemed to be his lot in life that he never accomplish anything quickly. Or at least nothing of any importance to him.

A young woman soon brought him a bowl of some indeterminate stew and a horn spoon. He scooped some into his mouth and swallowed, then paused, thinking about it. He decided it was better than what he had eaten at the fort, and as such, was edible. He wolfed down some more. When he was almost finished, he set the bowl down so the great Newfoundland could lap up the remains of it, including a few pieces of meat Barlow had deliberately left.

Minutes ticked by, but soon the pipe began making its way around the fire circle. When Barlow got it, he puffed in and blew some smoke to the four compass directions, as well as to Mother Earth and Father Sky, before passing the pipe to the next man.

Finally the ritual was over. "Now we parley," Two Hawks said in good English. "What's your name?"

"Will Barlow."

Two Hawks nodded. "Why've you come to our village, Will Barlow?"

"I was hopin' you boys might be able to help me a bit."

"We're friends to all the white-eyes," Two Hawks said earnestly. "We'll help if we can. Bloody right we will."

"You been spendin' too much goddamn time at Fort Hall," Barlow said, almost chuckling. The fact was obvious from the little he had heard of Two Hawks's speaking so far.

"Maybe yes, maybe no, goddammit!" Two Hawks said with a big grin. "How can we help?"

"You know any of the Shoshonis in these parts?" Barlow asked.

"Some," Two Hawks responded with a shrug. "Any of 'em in partic'lar?"

"I'm lookin' for a warrior by the name of White Bear. You know where I might find that ol' chil'?"

The men spoke quietly amongst themselves in their own language a few moments before Two Hawks said, "We don't know him."

"You certain?" Barlow asked anxiously, hopelessness beginning to well up in his chest.

Two Hawks nodded firmly. "Don't know him. Nope." He paused, then asked, "Why you lookin' for this bloody chap?"

"I been told he has my daughter. She ain't but a leetle gal. Only three years old. She was took from me by Umpquas over by the Great Water, and they lost her gamblin' to this White Bear."

Two Hawks shook his head slowly. "We don't know of no captives. No white captives." He suddenly seemed very nervous.

13

BARLOW SAT THERE, the hopelessness almost overpowering. While he had not expected to learn anything of value, he had foolishly allowed his hopes to build considerably. Now those hopes were dashed—again.

"You ain't even heard of any captives maybe in some Shoshoni camp?" he asked, almost desperately.

"Don't know of no bloody captives," Two Hawks insisted, still nervous. "Don't know if Shoshonis have captives. Don't know of no white captives."

It was too much, and Barlow began to suspect Two Hawks was hiding something. But what? *Did he really have Anna here?* Barlow wondered. *Could White Bear have lost her to Two Hawks and the Northern Paiutes somehow? Or had Red Cedar lied to me months ago and made up the name of White Bear and a visit by the Shoshonis to the Umpquas? Perhaps that was why no one out here, red or white, seems to have any idea of who White Bear is.*

Barlow sighed. He couldn't know the answer to any of these things, and it was unlikely that he would learn them. Not by directly asking, anyway. He decided he might have to stay in the vicinity and try to keep an eye on this band. Maybe that way he could learn if they were hiding something, and if that something was the presence of his daughter.

"Well, I'm obliged, Two Hawks, that you was willin' to parley with me." He let some of his despair show. "I was powerfully hopin' you'd know somethin'. Well, I reckon I'll be on my way. But since dark's nigh, you mind of I stay the night here? I'll be gone by first light."

"Yes. You stay. You'll be bloody damn good company." He tried to grin but didn't quite make it.

"Obliged again, Two Hawks," Barlow said evenly. Suddenly he asked, "Who was that warrior who brung me here?"

"Takin'-To-the-Sky," Two Hawks answered. "Why?"

"He needs to be taught some manners," Barlow said flatly. "He's too big for his britches, understand?"

Two Hawks nodded. "I understand. He's a bloody headstrong young man, but they're the best kind, wouldn't you say, dammit?"

"Reckon so. But one day it'll bring about his demise he don't learn to keep his arrogance under control." Barlow rose. "C'mon, Buffler." He passed out of the tipi and into the fading afternoon sunlight. It was still hotter than blazes, but the dark would bring a good coolness, he thought. With the Newfoundland at his side, he strolled back to his mules and unsaddled Beelzebub. He brushed the animal down, and then unloaded his now-meager amount of supplies. He had so few supplies these days that one mule could carry them all, so Barlow alternated between the two pack animals.

That done, he gathered a bit of wood and started a small fire. He had some meat left from a deer he had shot the day before. Despite the heat, it had not yet gone bad. He hung it on a stick over the fire and put some coffee on, using water from the thin trickle of a brook nearby. He also filled his two canteens. Finally he sat on the ground, stretching out to rest on one elbow, waiting for his food.

By the time he ate, it was almost fully dark. He sat

up, eating without much enthusiasm, sharing the half-raw deer meat with Buffalo. When the meat was gone, he pulled out his pipe, filled it and lit it. He puffed softly, occasionally sipping some coffee. "Somethin' about all this jist ain't right, boy," he said as he absentmindedly stroked the dog's big head. "I jist wish I could figure out what it was. Damn, if I don't feel plumb foolish at times like this."

With a long sigh, he tossed out the dregs from his coffee cup and knocked the last of the ashes from his pipe before putting it away. He pulled out his sleeping robe and stretched out on it, hands behind his head, trying to relax. It wasn't easy. But finally drowsiness began to drift over him. Then, just before the peace of sleep overcame him he heard something that snapped him upright. He wasn't sure what he had heard, but he knew it was important, out of the ordinary, and out of place for a poor Northern Paiute village. He sat there, straining to catch the sound again, or to decipher what it was he had heard.

Seconds turned into minutes, but whatever sound that had startled him was not made again. Still he sat, though, hoping to make some sense of it. Realization was slow in coming, but come it did. "Goddamn, Buffler," he whispered. "That was English I heard. Not much of it, but what there was of it was not spoke like an Injin speaks it."

He sat some more, trying to calm himself. Once he did, he could think more clearly. It had not been Anna's voice, of that he was certain. It was a male voice, though very young. He wondered if it could be . . . He would have to find out. And soon. He continued to sit, waiting until the camp was quiet. When he decided the time was right, he stood. Buffalo leaped up, tail wagging. The big dog knew there were doin's afoot. Barlow nodded at the Newfoundland and whispered, "C'mon, boy, time to find out what this secret is."

Barlow moved stealthily around the periphery of the village, Buffalo padding silently beside him, tongue loll-

ing. Barlow had only a vague idea of where the voice
had come from, which meant he had to check at least
half a dozen lodges. It would be no easy feat. He stopped
and knelt, patting Buffalo's neck as he thought this out.
He quickly realized that he could not just go about en-
tering lodge after lodge without getting caught. Since it
would be pitch dark inside each tipi, and he didn't really
know who or what he would be looking for, the chances
of finding out anything were almost nonexistent. What
he needed to do, he decided, was to somehow get everyone out of their lodges in a way that he could see them.
That wouldn't be easy either, but he would have to figure out how.

Discouraged, he headed back toward his little camp,
his thoughts focused. Suddenly he stopped. Then he
smiled into the darkness. He got his bearings, and then
headed for a particular lodge. He stopped there, and indicated with hand signals that Buffalo should stay there.
Then he slipped inside. Within a moment, he found what
he needed, and was back outside. Still silently, he hurried back to his little camp, where in the moonlight he
looked over the pistol he had taken from Taking-To-the-
Sky's lodge. He had seen the warrior carrying the pistol,
and it would, he thought, suit his purposes.

Barlow lay down and almost willed himself to relax
enough to fall asleep. His inner clock woke him when
he had wanted to wake—perhaps a half hour before
dawn was about to break. He swiftly went to the stream
and with a stick scooped out a hole. He turned and fired
the pilfered pistol into the air. Before the smoke had
cleared, he dropped the weapon in the hole, covered it
with mud and stomped it down. Then he ran like hell
toward his camp, and the village.

Paiutes were pouring out of their lodges in various
states of dress, searching frantically for the source of the
attack. Within minutes, they realized that there was
none, and they began heading back to their lodges, talking excitedly.

Barlow stood on the fringes, searching the people as

they moved about. He started when he saw a white boy, dressed in ragged clothes, being tugged none-too-gently toward one of the tipis. From the look he got of the boy, he was certain it was Georgie Skinner. The boy looked much like a miniature version of his father. Moments later, Barlow spotted a white child in the arms of a Paiute woman who was talking with some friends. Though he couldn't tell at this distance, Barlow was sure it had to be Sam Dockery Junior, Judith's young son.

He waited, watching intently as his anger rose, to see which lodge the children were taken to. The older boy was taken into one right away, but it was perhaps ten minutes before the woman holding the younger captive headed into a tipi—the same one.

Barlow stood there a while to allow his rage to dwindle to a manageable level. Since he had lost Anna to Indians, he could not bear to see children—particularly white children—being held captive in any Indian village. The very thought of it infuriated him. So now he had to calm down, and try to come up with a plan to get them back.

He downed some coffee and chewed on pieces of jerky, unsure of what he should do. He couldn't just go into that lodge, grab the youngsters and ride out, of course. He decided that his only recourse was to try to bargain for them, though he had almost nothing to trade. And then there was the little problem of Two Hawks having lied to him about knowing nothing of captives. It was no wonder the chief had been so secretive.

Barlow and Buffalo strode toward Two Hawks's lodge and called for entrance. When it was given—reluctantly—man and dog entered and sat. Though he was hungry, Barlow waved off the food that one of Two Hawks's wives tried to give him. He did accept some coffee. He took a few sips, and then said, without preliminary, "I saw two white captives here just a bit ago, ol' hoss. I want to take 'em out of here."

"You're bloody lyin'," Two Hawks said with a straight face.

"Buffler shit, hoss," Barlow snapped. "I just saw the two of 'em with my own eyes. You're a lyin' sack of shit, goddammit, and a disgrace to your people."

Two Hawks winced under the insults, but the only outward sign of anything he gave was a hardening of the eyes.

"Look, I don't expect you to just give over them young'ns to me. I'll offer you a fair ransom for 'em."

"What you got to give?" Barlow asked, interest flickering in his eyes.

"Not much," Barlow admitted ruefully. "Them two ol' mules of mine out there. A bit of powder and shot perhaps."

"You give me the dog," Two Hawks said firmly. "All three mules. And your rifle. That's a bloody damn good rifle."

"You can jist kiss my rosy red American ass, Two Hawks," Barlow said sharply, his anger threatening to explode. "You can have the two pack mules, plus I'll throw in the two horse pistols I got out there on my saddle. Plus powder and shot."

"All mules. And the rifle." He decided he did not want Buffalo once he had seen the way the big dog was looking at him.

"Two mules, two horse pistols," Barlow said, barely containing his rage. "And I'll tell you what, hoss, when I get them young'ns back to Fort Hall, I'll get you a fine rifle there, plus more shot and a heap of powder."

Two Hawks laughed, though it was a hollow sound. "I don't trust no bloody goddamn American," he said sharply.

"Listen you antelope-humpin' sack of shit," Barlow spit out, "I ain't ever lied to you, goddammit. You was the one who lied to me. Goddamn two-tongued, fish-eatin', goddamn son of a bitch."

Two Hawks looked as if he had just been slapped in the face, and now his anger grew. "Your rifle. Now!" he said, almost shouting. "All three mules. *And* the horse pistols!"

"Piss on you, Two Hawks."

"No trade," Two Hawks said with finality. "They stay here."

Barlow nodded sharply, knowing he would get nowhere with the Paiute now. "You best keep 'em safe from harm, hoss," he said tightly. "I aim to git back to Fort Hall and bring back some boys to take them children out of here. And if they ain't here when I git back, or it they've been harmed, I swear to you, goddammit, that I will lay this village to waste, and kill every goddamn man, woman and young'n I find here."

Two Hawks smiled slowly. "You best go now, you bloody, stupid bastard. You'll get no help from my friends at Fort Hall." He sounded arrogant, sure of himself.

"We'll jist see about that," Barlow said. He rose and stomped out, with an upset Buffalo at his side. The dog knew something was wrong, but couldn't, of course, discern what it was.

At his little camp, Barlow quickly loaded his supplies on one of the mules and then saddled Beelzebub. He was feeling a bit uncomfortable here, as the number of Paiutes watching him continued to grow. He could feel the hate emanating from them, and he wanted to be out of there in a hurry.

As he worked, though, he thought about what Two Hawks had said about the men at Fort Hall. If they were friends with Two Hawks and the Northern Paiutes, it would explain why they would not want to talk about white captives, or even quarter-breed captives. And it would explain their lack of assistance to him. Even if Anna was held by the Shoshonis, McTavish would know that any search party might come across bands of Northern Paiutes, and would therefore run the risk of seeing some captives that they might not be willing to ransom. They very well could leave the children here, preferring instead to keep on good terms with Two Hawks so that their trade was not interrupted. The very thought appalled Barlow.

Seething, Barlow rode out of the village soon after, half expecting an arrow in the back. He looked back once, when he was about a quarter of a mile away, and noted the small group of warriors following him at a discreet distance. He was so angry that he considered turning and firing at them. He was a good enough rifle shot to take down at least one of them at this distance. But that would not help Sam Junior and Georgie, and he had every intention of returning and getting those children out of the village and back to their parents.

He looked back again once more nearly half a mile after the first time. The warriors were no longer following him. He was relieved at that. He did not want a bunch of angry warriors trailing him wherever he went. And he did not plan to go back to Fort Hall just yet. No, he would not be going back there until he had the children safely out of the Paiute village.

Just how he was going to free them, he had no idea right now. But he knew he would come up with something. He would have to lay low for a while anyway, to let the Paiutes forget about him and his interest in the captive children. If he tried going back now to rescue the youngsters, the village would be wary, on the alert, and make his mission incredibly difficult, if not outright impossible. Still, he was dead certain that he would free them. It was just a matter of time, and he had plenty of that. Even finding Anna would have to wait for this one. There was no way he could leave those children in that village, knowing they were there. And not when he knew their kinfolk.

First, however, he had to find a place to hole up for a spell. He wanted to be far enough away from the Paiute village so he didn't have to worry about being found, but not so far away that he couldn't get back there in a day or so of riding. So it was a long day in the saddle for him, but he soon found a place where he thought he would be safe and out of the way.

14

WHILE BARLOW HOLED up for a few days, he had plenty of time to think, which was not always a good thing for him. However, this time it had some benefits, for the more he thought about the situation, the more he realized how tough it was going to be. These were not adult prisoners, ones he could just sneak in, find and lead out. They were children, the oldest only about five. He would not only have to find Georgie Skinner, but he would have to somehow convey, in the dark while trying not to wake anyone else, that he was there to help. And do it all without the lad giving them away either through fear or excitement.

If that weren't bad enough, there was Sam Junior. He was only seven or eight months old, and could do nothing to help himself. Indeed, Barlow hadn't thought of it until he had been in his lair for a couple of days, that he would have to take a Paiute woman with him to feed the child.

The more Barlow thought about it, the more impossible the task seemed to be, and after a few days, he began to wonder if he was being a fool for even considering such a seemingly hopeless endeavor.

Whenever such hopelessness crept up on him, though, he would picture little Anna in his mind. He would hope that no other man who saw her as a captive would let her stay there without at least trying to secure her release through whatever means possible. So he could not let Sam Junior and Georgie stay in that village. He had to do everything in his power to get them back, both for their sakes and for their parents' sakes, as well as Anna's sake, in some ways.

With the thoughts of Anna constantly renewing his determination to help the two boys being held by the Northern Paiutes, he began to cast around in his head for ways he could manage to accomplish it. He reconsidered his decision not to go to Fort Hall, thinking that perhaps he could force them into taking some kind of action, perhaps with George Skinner's backing. McTavish could not refuse him when Barlow had seen the children with his own eyes. Or could he? Barlow did not trust McTavish one bit, and he still suspected the factor was hiding something. And, since Skinner had not seen fit to report to McTavish that the two children were missing in the first place, trying to get him to demand some action was a long shot. No, Barlow decided, he would get no help at Fort Hall. This was a mission he would have to carry out on his own.

He discarded several ideas as either unworkable or downright foolish, and as time dragged on he grew more and more melancholy, until he was almost afraid to try anything at all. He sat there, back against a tree trunk, and he stared vacantly at the fire. He felt paralyzed; as if he couldn't move, even if he wanted to. His mind was a blank. He didn't even notice, really, when Buffalo started barking at him, pawing the ground near him and attacking him in a mock way, trying to get him to come to his senses. Barlow was oblivious to it all.

Confused, Buffalo pulled back a little, and lay his front half almost on the ground, with this back end sticking up. He growled a little, whined, and barked some more. When that brought no reaction from Barlow, the

Newfoundland moved up warily and lapped at his master's face. Then, throwing caution to the wind, the dog began pawing Barlow's chest with his big nails.

Barlow jerked out of his funk, and slapped the dog away from him. "What the hell're you doin', Buffler?" he said, pushing to his feet. He swayed a moment, dizzy at having stood so quickly after having been seated, unmoving for so long. He shook his head to clear it and looked around. It was almost dark. Had he sat there virtually the entire day, unmoving, unthinking? he wondered. He spit in the dirt, disgusted with himself. There was no other answer for it. He had to have done that.

Barlow knelt and called the dog to him. He stroked the fur over the dog's big head, and looked into the dark, caring eyes. "Well, good goddamn, if I ain't a shameful one, eh, Buffler?" he said softly. "Pissin' away the whole goddamn day frettin' over what I can't do. Well, you know what, boy? We are gonna get them young'ns out of that goddamn Paiute village, if I have to ride in there and fight the whole goddamn lot of 'em myself."

He stood, still petting Buffalo. He nodded. It was time to move on, time to do something about those youngsters. He had wasted more than enough time. There was no need for some great plan. He just had to figure out how to get in there, get the children and get back out again. Simple. Definitely not easy to accomplish, but simple. There was no room for fretting.

Barlow suddenly bellowed into the emptiness around him, a roar of annoyance, rage and determination. It drifted away in the wind, leaving a heavy silence, which lasted long enough for the birds to decide it was safe to start their singing again. Barlow laughed, rubbing his face and hair vigorously with his big hands, as if trying to stir up the life inside him. It seemed to work. "Tomorrow, Buffler," he said, almost happy now that he had decided it was time to act. "Come first light, me and you are goin' out to rescue them two youngsters from the clutches of the savages."

He slept well that night, the first time he had done so

since he had come to this small den of trees, brush and
slim thread of a brook. He awoke bursting with energy,
ready—and willing—to take on every Northern Paiute
in the world here and now if it would help free Sam
Junior and Georgie. He had a hasty meal of rabbit left
over from two days ago. It was getting a little ripe, but
he figured he would survive it. That and some coffee,
which he was getting close to being out of, made a fine
morning meal. Buffalo cleaned up the leftovers of rabbit,
trotted off to do his business, and then loped back to
camp, eager to be on the trail.

"Yeah, we're goin', boy," Barlow said to the dog,
grinning a little. "Soon's I get the mules ready and ol'
Beelzebub saddled up."

Neither task took very long, and as soon as they were
accomplished, Barlow pulled himself into the saddle. He
sat there a moment, breathing deeply a few times. "Well,
let's git movin', Buffler," he said with a laugh. "We ain't
got all the day for sittin' 'round doin' nothin'." He
heeled the big, blackish mule into motion and made sure
the animal kept up a steady, mile-eating walk.

He still had not seen the village, however, by the time
darkness started sweeping over him again. He shrugged,
a bit annoyed, and dismounted. He unsaddled the riding
mule and unloaded the one pack animal. He figured he
was fairly close to the village, but he was not sure how
far. The Northern Paiutes likely would have moved the
camp at least a few miles. It had looked—and smelled—
well used when he was there last, and they were about
due for a move. He figured they would have picked up
and traveled on a ways even if they had not had to for
sanitary reasons. He was sure that Two Hawks would
have been a little worried that Barlow might have really
gone to Fort Hall and was returning with some of the
traders. So he would have moved, just to be on the safe
side, Barlow decided.

Since he was certain he was not too far from the village, he decided a cold camp would be best. He wanted
coffee, but would have to do without. It was better that

he conserve what little he had left anyway.

Buffalo trotted off into the dusk and soon came back with a prairie dog in his jaws. Barlow assumed the dog had killed and eaten at least two others out there. He would not be satisfied with just the one.

Barlow had to content himself with water from his canteen and more jerky, which he was coming to hate. What he wouldn't give now for a big juicy slab of buffalo ribs oozing with hot grease. He smiled into the darkness. "Best not go dwellin' on such thoughts for too long, ol' hoss," he mockingly scolded himself quietly. Before long, he was asleep, lying on his robe, with the big dog pressed up against his back. Coyotes serenaded them to slumber.

Two hours' worth of riding the next morning brought him as close to the Northern Paiute village as he wanted to get in the daylight. Once again, he could see the vultures circling lazily in the sky a mile away. He shook his head at the strangeness of some things. The vultures were such striking birds when they were flying, their big wings catching the updrafts as they soared. They were graceful and beautiful. But close up, they were about the ugliest critters Barlow had ever seen. Faces that even a mother vulture would have trouble loving. And they were as ungainly as they were unsightly.

Soon after, moving forward slowly, Barlow could see the smoke from the lodge fires. He spotted a ridge off to the southwest a little, and he turned that way, until he was almost atop it. He dismounted and loosened the saddle. He ground-staked the three mules. Then, taking his rifle, a canteen, some jerky and his spyglass, he headed over the top of the big, rounded ridge and a little way down the other side. There he plunked himself. Buffalo lay down beside him.

With the village about a mile away, the telescope was of little use, though he could make out movement with it. He could not distinguish one figure from another, though, from this distance, so he soon gave up on it and just sat. It was going to be a long day.

Barlow napped off and on, nodding out from the heat and the boredom, trusting to Buffalo to wake him if anyone approached. Once in a great while he would check the village through the collapsible telescope, just to see if there was anything unusual taking place. There wasn't. As far as he could tell, everything was as normal as could be down in the village.

After what seemed like several eternities, dusk started slipping over the land, slowly spreading yard by yard. Barlow continued sitting there until full darkness had come, though there was still a fair amount of light from the moon and the stars.

Finally Barlow stood. "Time to go, boy," he said quietly to the dog. He and the Newfoundland crested the ridge, where Barlow tightened the saddle on Beelzebub. Then he rode off, Buffalo walking alongside, the two pack mules following quietly, heeding the tugging of the rope that Barlow held.

He stopped within a dozen yards of one of the lodges, next to a couple of straggly trees. He tied the mules and said, "Buffler, you stay here. Stay and watch over Beelzebub and the other animals."

The dog made some funny sounds, indicating that he did not like being left behind, but Barlow knew the Newfoundland would obey. Barlow slung his rifle across his back by the rawhide sling, and headed away on foot, moving, as he always did, silently, a shadow among the shadows. He stopped at the nearest tipi and let his breathing slow, checking out the area around him with all his senses. The village appeared to be asleep, so he moved off again, heading for the tipi where Georgie and Sam Junior had been kept. A chill suddenly snaked up his spine as he thought that perhaps the Paiutes had moved them, or even traded them to another band. He tried to shake off the feeling, hoping they were still being kept in the same lodge.

He found the right tipi, and he paused outside, listen-

ing intently. All he heard from inside were snores and
the unconscious shuffling of sleeping bodies. He pulled
the flap open just enough to allow him to slip inside,
and then he stopped again, letting his eyes adjust to the
deeper darkness inside the lodge. Then creeping along
on all fours, he began looking for the children. He saw
Sam Junior, but decided to keep searching. It made more
sense to him to get Georgie out first.

It seemed agonizingly slow, but Barlow finally found
the older captive, and was thankful that the boy was
sleeping by himself. He looked forlorn in the dim light
from the faded fire. All he had for a bed was a poor
blanket, rather than a nice thick buffalo robe like many
others might have. On the other hand, from what Barlow
had seen of this village, very few people had much in
the way of amenities. They were a poor, shabby tribe
all in all.

Barlow stopped next to the boy and waited a few seconds, making sure no one had been disturbed. Then he
struck, fast, one hand slapping across the boy's mouth,
the other hand pressing gently on his chest to keep him
down. Barlow bent over and whispered, "I'm here to
save you, boy. Keep quiet. Understand?" He trusted in
the boy's being at least somewhat calmed by hearing
English as spoken by a white man.

The petrified Georgie nodded fearfully.

Still speaking directly into the lad's ear, Barlow said,
"I'm gonna slip out. You lay here and count to ten—
five times. Can you do that?" When Georgie nodded
once more, Barlow added, "Then you come outside. Understand?"

Georgie was still scared to death, but he had relaxed
a little. He nodded again.

"Good." Then Barlow slipped away. He moved relatively quickly, and moments later he was outside. He
squatted just to the side of the lodge's entrance flap, and
wiped the sweat from his brow on a sleeve. It was almost
cool outside, but the heat inside the lodge had been sti-
fling.

Barlow had a hand on the hilt of his knife when he heard faint sounds from inside the tipi. Then a scared Georgie Skinner stepped out, and saw Barlow. He stopped, not sure what to do. Barlow smiled at him and held out his hand. The boy tentatively took it, and Barlow tugged him close. "I know your ma and pa, Georgie," he whispered. "And I've come to take you back to them."

Georgie's eyes brightened. But then he asked solemnly, "What about Sam Junior?"

"I aim to git him, too, son. Don't you fret. First, we're gonna git you out of here. You ready?"

"Yessir," Georgie said, wide-eyed.

Barlow scooped the boy up in one arm. As he started walking toward where he had left the mules, he said softly, "My name's Will Barlow. Did them Injins mistreat you any?"

"Some," Georgie said, trying to sound brave about it. "But wasn't so bad."

"That's good. Now, I got me a few mules out yonder. I'll leave you there while I come back here for Sam Junior."

"I'm afraid," Georgie said.

"I reckon you are, boy. And that's all right. You'll be safe, though. My partner will watch over you."

"Partner?"

"Yep. He's there, and he'll watch over you real good. Now, I got to ask you something. What's the name of the Paiute woman who's tendin' to Sam Junior?"

"Coyote Woman." He giggled a little. "That's a funny name for a person."

"It sure is," Barlow agreed.

They arrived at the mules, and Barlow set Georgie down. "Where's your partner?" the boy asked.

"Right here," Barlow said, petting Buffalo's big head. The dog's tail was whipping back and forth.

"He's a dog!"

"That's right. And the best dog you'll ever meet. This

here dog plumb shines, boy. His name's Buffler. And he'll watch over you good. You hungry?"

"Yep." Georgie looked skeptically at Buffalo, still not sure about the huge dog.

"You go on and pet him," Barlow said. "It'll be all right." He grabbed a few pieces jerky from his packs and handed them to the boy. "Sorry, son, but that's all I got for fillin' your meatbag."

"You talk funny," Georgie said, giggling a bit.

"Reckon I do sometimes, boy. Now you share a little of that there jerky with Buffler. He'll keep good watch over you. I'll be back soon's I can with Sam Junior, and then we'll mosey on up to Fort Hall, where your folks'll be waitin' for you."

"All right." The boy seemed determined to be big and strong.

15

BARLOW SWIFTLY RETRACED his steps into the village and to the lodge. He slipped inside again, more sure of himself this time. Once more he stopped inside to let his heartbeat slow and to let his eyes adjust. Everything still seemed normal to him, which was a relief. He again scrabbled slowly, silently forward until he stopped where Sam Junior lay sleeping in the arms of a plump young woman.

Pausing a few moments to make sure everything was still normal, he then did to the woman what he had done to Georgie—slapped a hand over her mouth and another on her chest, keeping her down. He bent over her and whispered right into her ear, "I'm takin' the boy, and you'll come with us, Coyote Woman."

Startled, she shook her head as much as she was able to under the pressure of his huge, powerful hand. In the dim glow of the embers, deep fear was reflected in her eyes.

"You will, or I'll cut your throat. And then I'll kill everyone else in this lodge." There was no mistaking the conviction in his voice.

The woman nodded as best she could, and seemed to calm down a little.

"If you make any sound at all, I'll cut your goddamn heart out and feed it to the wolves. Understand?"

Coyote Woman tensed again, but nodded.

Leaving his hand on her mouth for the time being, he used his other hand to place the loop of the rawhide rope he had prepared earlier over her head and then tightened the loop against her throat. "Get the chil' and let's go." He rose, tugging lightly on the rope. One good yank and he would cut off her air almost instantly, and she knew it.

Coyote Woman picked up the cradleboard with the still sleeping infant, and they both tiptoed across the lodge and outside, where Coyote Woman stopped just long enough to hang the cradleboard on her back.

Barlow waited impatiently until she was done, and then headed toward his camp, towing the woman with him. He walked at a good clip, fueled by a sense of urgency to be far away from this place. Once there, Buffalo came bounding out, happy to see his master. Georgie was awed that Barlow had actually returned—and had brought Sam Junior with him.

"You think you can ride by yourself, boy?" Barlow asked.

Georgie nodded, determined to show he was a big boy.

"Good." Barlow grabbed him, and almost tossed him atop the mule with the supplies after tossing a piece of fur on the pack saddle to give it some illusion of comfort. The packs hanging from the diagonal wood uprights of the saddle would help keep Georgie in place.

Barlow took the rope from around Coyote Woman's neck. "Remember what I said," he snapped at her. "I got no love for any people who steal children away from their folks. Seein' as you're one of 'em, I'd not hesitate to carve you into pieces and feed you to Buffler there. That clear to you?"

Coyote Woman nodded, still terrified.

Barlow didn't know if she really understood all his words. He still had no clue as to how much English she spoke or understood, but he figured she got enough of it simply by his tone and manner.

Barlow helped her onto the other pack mule and swiftly fashioned a makeshift rein for her and one for Georgie. He mounted Beelzebub, and said, "Let's go."

Coyote Woman rode out first, knowing Barlow would not let her ride behind him. Georgie followed her, simply because his mule was used to following the other. Then Barlow came along, Buffalo loping alongside Beelzebub. Barlow rode to the head of the line almost and swatted Coyote Woman's mule on the rump. The animal brayed, though not too loudly, and picked up its pace. When it did, Barlow faded back to the rear, keeping a frequent watch over his shoulder.

At the pace they kept up, by the time dawn started poking its rosy glow over the hills to the east, they were at the place where Barlow had holed up. He decided to stop. Georgie was falling asleep as he rode, they were all hungry, and the mules needed rest. He risked being heard and shot a small deer just before getting to the campsite. Soon a fire was going, meat was roasting and coffee was heating. Georgie curled up and slept. Coyote Woman sat stern-faced and angry, letting Sam Junior suckle at her ample breasts.

Barlow glanced at Coyote Woman. He decided that if she were not a Northern Paiute—or at least not a Northern Paiute from this particular band—he might find her of some interest. She was somewhat handsome of face, but rather too plump for his taste. Still, having not had the pleasures of a woman since the night before he and the wagon had gotten to Fort Hall, he might have considered it. If only she wasn't a member of this particular band of Northern Paiutes.

He soon ate, after which he sipped coffee, feeling the scratch of fatigue in his eyes. The heat of the day, even though he was in the shade, only added to his tiredness. He wanted nothing more than to sleep right at the moment, but he was not sure that would be wise. Still, the animals could use more rest, as could the children. But they could not stay here very long. The absence of Coyote Woman and the two captives would have been noticed a little while ago, and the Paiutes were almost certainly coming after them. He knew they would have to ride hellbent if they were to keep ahead of the Indians and reach Fort Hall safely. But a little more rest would be good for them all.

Barlow allowed himself to doze. He was not concerned about Coyote Woman running off. Buffalo would make sure that she stayed where she was. Besides, she was even more tired than he was, he figured. Just before sleep overtook him, he cracked his eyes. The Paiute woman had stretched out on the ground, cradling the sated and now fast-asleep Sam Junior.

He awoke three hours later. As he knelt to stir up the fire and put more meat to roasting he could still feel the fatigue clinging to him like the veneer of sweat from the hot day. "Goddamn, Buffler," he said with a wry grin that came more from annoyance than humor, "I'm gittin' to old for such doin's."

Barlow gave the meat barely long enough to get hot on the outside, while still tepid at best inside. But he didn't care. Right now he needed strength and energy. He ate quickly, quietly, sharing a little with the big dog. When he was done, he wiped his greasy hands on his tattered osnaburg shirt. He looked at the garment, and at his buckskin pants. The trousers were black with grease and smoke and blood. The shirt was not as fouled, but was far more worn, and looked as if it would fall apart at any moment. Even his moccasins were showing definite signs of wear. He would have to see if he could work a bit at Fort Hall, as much as he hated the thought, so he could scrape up enough money to get himself a new outfit. He went on much longer and he'd be roaming around out here naked, he figured.

He went over and none too gently kicked Coyote Woman in the side. She mumbled and grumbled, but finally sat up, leaning back against a small boulder. "We leave now?" she asked.

"Directly," Barlow said. "There's meat on the fire. Eat. You may not git a chance to do so again for a spell."

The woman nodded, but she looked troubled.

"Somethin' botherin' you, woman?" Barlow asked.

Coyote Woman appeared to be mighty reluctant to say anything, and Barlow was in no mood to try to figure it out, so he shrugged and turned back toward the fire. Suddenly he realized what the problem was. He turned back. "You need to go in the bushes?" he asked bluntly.

Coyote Woman nodded.

"Go on and go. But don't you try runnin'. Go with her, Buffler."

The Paiute looked displeased with that, but she stalked off behind a screen of bushes, the Newfoundland following at a discreet distance. Before long the two were back, and Coyote Woman went to the fire and squatted alongside it. She reached for the knife at her belt, and froze, suddenly looking nervously at Barlow. He nodded, and she pulled it carefully out and sliced off some chunks of the deer meat and placed them on a small piece of bark. She went back to the boulder and sat, eating silently but with a hearty appetite, and keeping an eye on Sam Junior, who was still slumbering in his cradleboard.

Barlow roused Georgie, which took some doing. The five-year-old just did not want to wake. Barlow couldn't blame him, but they had to get moving, so he had little pity for the child right now. Finally Georgie was mostly awake, and Barlow gave him some of the deer meat on a piece of bark. It took a few minutes, but the boy soon began eating. When he finished, he was a lot more alert.

Coyote Woman pulled Sam Junior out of the cradleboard and tossed away the grass that become fouled by absorbing the tot's wastes. She cleaned the boy off and the found some fresh grass to pack into the cradleboard with the child. She slung the cradleboard across her back, and perched precariously on the boulder to wait while Barlow kicked some dirt over the fire.

Barlow helped Coyote Woman onto the one pack mule and lifted Georgie onto the other one. Then he climbed into his saddle, and they all began moving, Coyote Woman first again, Georgie behind and to the side of her. Barlow stayed a few paces back to keep an eye on both of them, as well as watch their back trail.

Barlow pushed them as hard as he dared. He had no idea how far behind them the Paiutes were, but he knew they were back there and would be coming fast. A few miles from the camp, he turned them more easterly than northerly. He hoped that in doing so—which would take them away from Fort Hall—he would fool the pursuing warriors. He figured they would assume he would run straight for the fort and its safety. By taking a more circuitous route, he hoped to throw them off. It was a risk, he knew. The Paiutes could head straight toward the fort and be waiting for him when he swung back that way. But he had to take the chance. If he did not have two children—one only an infant—he would have made the run to the fort on a beeline, moving as fast as the animals could carry them. But they were not adults, and he would have to travel more slowly. Going in a roundabout direction was the best thing he could think of.

He finally allowed a stop just about the time that full darkness spread over them. He was lucky to have found a spot with a pitiful puddle for a water hole and some trees. He helped Coyote Woman and Sam Junior off the mule and let the Paiute woman take care of her needs, as well as the youngster's.

Then Barlow went to get Georgie, who was practically asleep though he was still sitting upright on the mule. Barlow lifted him in his arms and carried him to a comfortable spot and set him down. He brushed the hair back from the child's forehead. "Sleep well, boy," he said quietly. He was quite proud of Georgie. The boy had made the long, hard ride without complaint, though

Barlow knew he was suffering from the heat, the lack of sleep, the ride, fear and more.

Barlow was too tired to worry about food, even though he had shot another deer that afternoon. Right now, he didn't care. He did what he had to—unloaded the small amount of supplies, unsaddled Beelzebub and tended all three mules, and then spread his otter skin sleeping robe out. As he stepped behind a bush to relieve himself, he could feel the exhaustion dragging heavily on his shoulders. Done, he stood there a moment, listening. He heard nothing out of the ordinary. He finally went and lay down. Buffalo sprawled out next to him, his back brushing Barlow's side. Barlow was asleep in seconds. He was still not worried about Coyote Woman. She knew the dog would attack her if she tried anything against Barlow, and that the Newfoundland would alert Barlow if she tried to take one of the mules and run.

Coyote Woman had considered both those things, but she had come to the conclusion Barlow had known she would. She was becoming less afraid now. While Barlow had not exactly been friendly toward her, he had not treated her poorly either. That had surprised her, though she still did not doubt he would do whatever he thought necessary to save himself and the two young white boys. She did wonder why he had not made advances toward her. From all she knew, that was about the only thing white men thought Indian women were good for. She did not want to admit to herself the bit of sadness she felt at that. He was an attractive man, and so powerfully built. She wondered what kind of lover he would be, and had to fight back a giggle. No white man knew how to treat a woman. Everyone knew that.

Morning came much too soon for Barlow. The sun beating down on him through the stunted trees woke him, and he sat up groggily. He was sweating like a beast already. He didn't care that summer was having its last real fling before autumn start creeping in. It was just too damn hot, and he was tired of it. He stood.

Coyote Woman was awake and had stirred up the fire
and was cooking meat—and a pot of coffee. She was
bent over, adding some sticks to the fire when she realized he was watching her. She looked at him, somewhat nervously. "You no mind?" she asked, her voice
rich, though heavily accented.

"Mind what?"

"I get coffee from your pack. I make."

"No, I don't mind," he said, wiping sweat off his forehead with one sleeve. "It's good."

Coyote Woman went back to tending the fire. Barlow
checked on Georgie, who was still peacefully sleeping.
Barlow decided to wait a bit before waking the boy. Sam
Junior was awake and seemed happy in his cradleboard.

Barlow took care of his personal needs and then went
to the fire. He grabbed some meat and a mug of coffee
and sat back in the shade a little. As hot as it was, he
wanted no part of the fire right now. When he was done,
he woke Georgie. While the boy ate, Barlow loaded the
supplies on the mule that Georgie would continue to
ride, and then saddled Beelzebub. By the time he was
done, Georgie had finished eating, and everyone was
ready to move.

Barlow continued to push them hard throughout that
day, stopping once more only after dark. Another short
night and they were back on the trail again, traveling as
fast as Barlow thought they could without killing the
animals. He also swung them back northwestward, once
more angling toward Fort Hall. He called it a night in
late afternoon, not wanting to, but knowing he could not
push Georgie any more. Coyote Woman was beyond
exhaustion, though she would go as long as necessary,
he knew.

Morning brought a renewal of their dash across the
increasingly mountainous terrain. As he had all along,
Barlow kept a regular watch behind him, and sometime
just before noon, he thought he could see trails of dust
in the sky, and he knew their time was almost up. He
kept an eye out, looking for a place to make a stand,

trying to judge the speed at which the pursuers were coming up on them. An hour after he had first noticed they were being followed, he galloped ahead of Coyote Woman and turned her and Georgie toward a small stand of trees, boulders and a large deadfall.

16

IN A RUSH, Barlow pulled Georgie off his mule and shoved him down where several dead trees had fallen against a medium-sized boulder. It was, Barlow figured, about the safest spot here. "You, too, Coyote Woman," Barlow commanded, pointing next to Georgie.

When the woman had hunkered down there with Sam Junior still in the cradleboard, Barlow said, "Anything happens to them two young'ns, I'll have your hair. Understand?"

Coyote Woman nodded. She was not too afraid. She did not think he would do what he threatened. But she was not about to harm the children anyway. If she saw a chance to flee to the safety offered her by the Paiute warriors, she would take it, and bring either or both of the boys with her. She had claimed the younger boy to replace the infant son she had lost to sickness half a year ago. Still, if there was a battle, which seemed certain now, she would be in as much danger as Barlow as long as bullets and arrows were flying about.

Barlow knelt behind several downed trees. One had fallen partially atop a couple of others, making a pretty formidable barrier, yet there was a gap just big enough

for him to shoot through. He stuck his rifle through the
natural shooting port. On the log right in front of his,
he placed his two horse pistols and his two belt pistols.
His powder horn, buckskin sack of lead balls and a
smaller pouch of caps were within reach. Then he
waited, occasionally glancing at Buffalo, who was lying
a few feet to his left.

Finally he spotted the mounted warriors moving toward him at a fast walk. When they were still two hundred yards away, he drew a bead on one and fired. He
swiftly reloaded, with practiced competence. When he
was done, the haze of powder smoke had cleared and
Barlow noted that the warrior was nowhere to be seen,
and there was one riderless pony.

Barlow aimed and fired again, and another Paiute warrior went down. Barlow quickly reloaded, figuring he
had time for at least one more shot before they were too
close for the rifle to be of much use. But when he got
ready to take that shot, he found that the Paiutes had
darted off into the trees and did not present a decent
target. Though the trees lining the makeshift trail were
not that thick, the shade and brush made it difficult to
pick out anything for certain. Barlow could see movement, but he could not tell man from horse at this distance.

He half stood for a better look, but decided that was
pure foolishness when an arrow thudded into one of the
logs to his left. He dropped back down to his knee. And
waited some more. It was, he thought, going to be a
long, unpleasant afternoon.

As the day dragged on and on, Barlow grew more
worried and more angry. He began to think that the Paiutes were going to wait until dark—or shortly before
full dark—and then sneak up on him, Coyote Woman,
and the two boys. He would be in deep trouble then.
With daylight, he could hold them off from a distance,
or even stand a fair chance if they all came at him at
once. But in the dark, he would be lost. Furious, he
poked the rifle through the logs and fired at the first thing

that he saw move back in the trees across from him. There was a crash from over there, but Barlow did not know whether he had hit a warrior or a horse. Not that he cared either way. Just hitting *something* was enough for now.

Still, he knew he could not just sit there forever, until they gained even more of an advantage than they already had through sheer numbers. And, the only way he figured he could do that was to go out there and attack them instead of waiting for them to come at him. Of course, if he left here, he would be more vulnerable, and he would leave Coyote Woman on her own, more or less, with nothing to keep her here. Except for Buffalo. He sighed, making up his mind. It was the only way.

"Georgie, come on over here boy," Barlow ordered. "Crawl on the ground, nice and low."

The boy did so, and Barlow rubbed his hair. "You done good, Georgie." He looked out across the way. Nothing seemed different. He looked back to the lad. "I'm goin' out there and pay them Paiutes a visit. I reckon I can discourage 'em from loiterin' in these parts lookin' to 'cause us more trouble."

"Ain't that gonna be scary?" the boy asked, wide-eyed.

"Reckon it might be some scary," Barlow admitted. "But it's gotta be done, son."

Georgie nodded, solemn.

"And while I'm gone," Barlow continued, "I need you to see to things here. Think you can do that, boy?"

Georgie nodded again, even more serious.

"Good, son. Now, I'm gonna leave Buffler here to help you out. He'll keep an eye out on Coyote Woman over there, and Sam Junior, and make sure they don't go wanderin' off and maybe git hurt. I'm gonna leave my rifle right here where it's at, and I expect you to watch over it. Don't you go messin' with it, though. Not unless them red devils come runnin' right up here and look to do you some harm."

"Yessir," Georgie said. He was proud that he had been given such an important task.

Barlow stuffed his two belt pistols away, hung his powder horn over his shoulder and dropped the pouches of shot and caps back into his shooting bag hanging over his other shoulder. Then he took the two horse pistols in hand. "Buffler, you stay here and watch out for things, boy." He glanced pointedly at Coyote Woman.

The Paiute nodded almost imperceptibly. She had gotten the message—Buffalo was being left behind to make sure she did not flee, or harm Sam Junior.

Barlow slipped away, keeping low, into the trees where the mules were tied. He gave no thought to warning the boy to do anything if he didn't come back, in large part because he never considered the possibility that he wouldn't come back. He headed deeper into the trees, and then angled southwest for roughly a quarter of a mile. He swung westward, and cut across the trail— which he assumed had been there for years, as a sort of Indian highway—into the trees again, and then began working his way north and a little east, heading toward where he figured the Paiutes had decided to roost while they waited him out.

He eased his pace as he neared the area where he thought the warriors would be. Soon after, he heard faint voices, which grew louder as he moved along. Finally Barlow stopped, letting his senses investigate the nearby world. He concluded that a group of them—perhaps all of them—were gathered in one spot. He guessed that there were at least one or two others away from the main group keeping a watch over where Barlow was supposed to be holed up.

Barlow swung to his left, moving silently, carefully through the trees and brush, eyes and ears searching. He found no one after several minutes, so he retraced his steps and then checked the other way. Again, he found no one. He nodded, and pressed on the way he had been going originally. He slowed more and more, until he was inching along, half bent over to make himself less visible. The voices were quite clear, being very close now. And he finally stopped behind a large cottonwood. Only ten or twelve feet in front of him, in a small open spot, sat seven Paiute warriors in a semicircle, facing away from him. They were talking softly, some smoking pipes, one or two chewing on jerky.

They were, to Barlow's eyes, poor excuses for warriors. He was glad they were not Shoshonis, who were much superior fighting men. These Paiutes, though, were like their village—shabby, wretched, well-worn and abused by their harsh life. Not that they could be discounted completely, but they were far from the caliber of Shoshonis or Sioux or Crows. Still, Barlow would have his hands full. Worse, he could really see only one way out of this, and he did not like what he would have to do.

He knew, however, that it was the only way to save not only himself but the two boys. Barlow steeled himself. It helped by remembering that these warriors had attacked the Skinner wagon, killed Simon Skinner, and stole Georgie Skinner and Sam Dockery Junior. They had tried to kill him before and would kill the two boys without compunction.

Drawing in a deep breath, and then letting it out slowly, Barlow stepped from behind the tree and walked quietly toward the men. Three paces from the tree, he fired both horse pistols, one after the other. Two warriors went down, and the others began to move, but they were not that fast. Before they could turn around and face him, he had tossed the two horse pistols aside and grabbed the other two pistols from his belt. He fired those, too, knocking down two more Paiutes.

The three remaining warriors charged toward him, pulling knives or war clubs. Barlow ducked one of the latter, came back up and smashed the man in the mouth with the barrel of his pistol. The warrior stumbled into a friend, and both fell to the ground.

The third Paiute, however, lashed out with his knife, slicing a thin furrow across the ribs on Barlow's left

side. Blood welled up and out, staining his shirt, but
Barlow did not notice the blood nor the pain. He
snapped out his left arm, and clipped the warrior on the
side of the head with a pistol, making the Paiute miss
as he attempted to stab his white foe again.

Almost by instinct, Barlow whipped halfway around
and jerked an elbow out. A Paiute howled as his nose
shattered, but Barlow had no time to follow up, as the
one he had knocked down a moment before was coming
at him again, knife extended. Barlow spun, trying to
keep away from the bloodstained knife, but was only
partly successful. The blade sliced across his side less
than an inch from the other wound. He slammed the
Indian in the side of the head with the outside of his
forearm, a powerful blow that sent the Paiute sprawling
to the ground, dazed.

Barlow whirled to face the other two warriors, and in
the doing managed to catch a war club on the top of his
left shoulder. Had he not been moving, it would have
splintered his head. The stroke carried the warrior into
Barlow, almost knocking him down, but he managed to
keep his feet. He dropped both pistols and slammed a
powerful punch to the Paiute's stomach, then followed
with a hard knee to his face when the warrior bent over
from the blow.

Barlow whipped out his knife and sank the blade to
the hilt in the Indian's stomach, just under the dia-
phragm. He twisted it as he pulled it free, trying to do
as much damage as possible.

The warrior fell to the ground and curled up, holding
his stomach, which was gushing blood.

Barlow glanced around and saw the warrior he had
first hit in the mouth with a pistol running toward the
ponies a few yards away, yelling wildly. In moments,
two more Paiutes had appeared near the horses. All three
of them jumped onto mounts and kicked them into a
dead run straight off, heading for the trail in the direction
of their village.

Slowly, Barlow checked on the Paiutes laying scattered around this makeshift camp. The one he had stabbed was not dead, but would not last long. The same was true of one of the men he had shot. He did not worry about them. The only one that showed any signs of real life was the warrior he had smashed in the face with his elbow.

Barlow looked down at the Paiute. Part of him wanted to let the man go, to stop the killing here. But another part of him raged yet at what this warrior and his friends had done—or tried to do. And when he thought of Georgie and Sam Junior being raised as virtual slaves in a piss-poor Northern Paiute village, his mind was made up. He knelt and swiftly plunged his knife into the warrior's chest.

He rose slowly, suddenly beginning to feel the aching of his wounds, and the tiredness that came as the adrenaline in his bloodstream subsided. But there was much to be done yet. First, he retrieved all four pistols and reloaded them. His belt pistols were returned to their rightful places, the two horse pistols he set down in a clean spot.

Then he made a quick, though thorough search of the area. He saw no one else, and with the number of ponies, he was sure all the Paiutes were accounted for. Finally, he took each body and tied it to the back of a Paiute pony. He figured that he had beaten the Paiutes soundly enough that they would not want to come after him again, but if they were considering pursuing him, this gesture might make them change their minds. Most other white men in his position would have scalped the Indians and left their bodies there for the scavengers. Barlow didn't think that it would hurt trying to see that the bodies got back to their people more or less intact. It would cost him nothing to make the gesture, and could possibly be of benefit to him.

It took a while, but at last he walked the ponies out to the trail, and swatted them, sending them on their way. Hopefully they would find their way home, or catch up to the other warriors some time. Barlow didn't care which. He had done what he could. The rest was up to the spirits.

Barlow retrieved his horse pistols and took another quick look around. Seeing no one, he headed back to his makeshift redoubt, taking a slightly roundabout way just to make sure none of the Paiutes had snuck over that way.

Buffalo was, of course, the first to know he was coming, and the big dog bounded up, tail wagging furiously. Barlow stopped for a moment and petted the Newfoundland before moving into the small haven.

"Well," Barlow said easily, "looks like you done a right good job, Georgie. You all right?"

"Yessir." The boy looked scared, but smiled at the praise.

"How about you, Coyote Woman? You and Sam Junior all right?"

"Yes," the woman said, rising with a little difficulty from the long day spent huddled on the ground. She picked up Sam Junior's cradleboard, and moved stiffly off a little ways and changed the grass in it.

Barlow tightened the saddle on Beelzebub, grabbed his rifle, and mounted the mule. "I'll be back directly," he announced. "We'll stay the night here. Git a fire goin'. I aim to return with meat."

He was true to his word, and was soon back with a deer carcass. He swiftly butchered it and set meat to roasting on the fire Coyote Woman had started. Only then did he unsaddle and tend to Beelzebub, and care for the two pack mules.

The deer meat was welcome, but the last of the coffee went into the pot. By going easy on it now, Barlow figured there would be enough for one decent cup each the next morning for him and Coyote Woman. The thought did not please Barlow at all.

After eating, Barlow allowed Coyote Woman to bandage the wounds on his sides with a few strips of blanket he carried with him. The blood had coagulated, and they had nothing to poultice them with, so Coyote Woman could do little more than wash them off a bit and then wrap them.

Then, with not much else to do, they all turned in early, tired from the long, tedious day.

Breakfast was a perfunctory affair, after which Barlow saddled Beelzebub, then loaded what few supplies he had left on the one mule and helped Georgie onto it. He finally assisted Coyote Woman onto the other mule, and they rode out.

17

FEELING FAIRLY CONFIDENT that the Northern Paiutes would not come after them again, Barlow did not press so hard. Not that he made a slow march across the mountainous country. He rode at a nice steady pace that would cover the miles in good time without wearing out the animals or the humans. He called earlier halts for the night, and did not insist on leaving by first light. He hunted more, so they always had fresh meat around, which helped them all keep up their strength. It would not have been a bad journey at all were it not for the fact that the two boys had been Indian captives, a not-too-friendly Coyote Woman was along, and there was no coffee.

However, it was only another five days before they began seeing indications that they were drawing near to the fort—more people, telltale signs of plenty of traffic, both foot and animal, various noises of industry floating faintly toward them. Sometime in the afternoon, they arrived in the direct vicinity of the fort. Barlow skirted the post at first, traveling instead to where the Skinner party had had their camp when he had left here. They were not there, but another group was. Barlow stopped his mule near a tall, rugged-looking man who had a full beard and a face that indicated he was not a cheerful man.

"Afternoon," Barlow said wearily.

The man nodded. He said nothing, though he did remove his hat and swipe a sleeve across his sweaty forehead.

"There was a party here a few weeks ago. Some folks named Skinner and some called Dockery. You know where they went?"

"Can't say as I do, Mister," the man said diffidently.

"You know anything?"

The man missed the insult. "Nope."

"Talkative ol' chil' aren't you?" Barlow muttered. "Obliged," he said aloud.

Minutes later, the pitiful little procession rode through the wide wood doors of the small trading fort.

The place was, as usual, bustling with activity. Barlow stopped in front of the factor's headquarters—a relatively shabby looking place, at least compared with the headquarters occupied by Dr. John McLoughlin at Fort Vancouver.

As Barlow dismounted, the prissy clerk, Ian Buxton, came out of the office. Barlow spotted him and said, "I'd be obliged if you'd tell Mr. McTavish I got to talk to him."

"Mr. McTavish is a busy man, Mr. Barlow," Buxton sniffed. "He has no time for the likes of you."

"That right?" Barlow said. He was tired and hungry; his clothes were tattered and barely hanging on him. He was frustrated at not having come close to finding Anna, and he did not want to deal with a mealy-mouth prig like Ian Buxton.

"That is a fact, Mr. Barlow."

Barlow grabbed him by the fancy shirtfront and jerked him to the side. Buxton fell in the dirt, bouncing on a pile of mule manure before scrambling up looking disgusted. He was about to protest most vehemently when he noticed that Buffalo was moving toward him. He decided speeches could wait until later.

"Don't ever git in my way agin, boy," Barlow warned. He turned and pulled Georgie from the mule and helped Coyote Woman down. Then, he walked toward the factor's office. He tried the door, but it was locked. In his low humor, Barlow was enraged. He took a few steps back and bolted forward, slamming into the wood door with his massive shoulder. The door sagged, but held. Barlow backed up and rammed it again. This time the jamb splintered and the door almost fell. From there it was simply a matter of one good kick and the door was on the floor.

"Well, c'mon," Barlow said to Coyote Woman, Buffalo and Georgie. He waited while the boy and the Paiute, carrying Sam Junior, tentatively entered the building. The dog had no hesitation, and just marched in, tail waving slowly, nose taking in all the new scents.

Barlow shoved forward, down the little hallway to the office at the end on the right side.

Finan McTavish sat at his desk, terrified. He had heard the commotion and when he heard Barlow's voice, he had gotten scared. "Mister Barlow!" McTavish said with false joviality. " 'Tis good to have ye back."

"You're as piss poor a liar as you are a manager of this tradin' post, McTavish," Barlow growled.

McTavish blinked a few times, fighting back the anger that would only hurt him if he allowed it to show. "What can I do for ye, Mister Barlow. I have many tasks and canna spare the time for chatting."

"Where're the Skinners?" Barlow demanded.

McTavish shrugged. "Gone."

"Gone where?"

"I dunna know, lad. They left here aboot two weeks after ye did. They were heading west. Mister Skinner said they had to press on for the Oregon country."

"While their children were still in the clutches of those savages?" Barlow asked, a little surprised.

McTavish shrugged again. "I canna say what was in

their heads, Mr. Barlow, but I think they thought they would ne'er see their children again. That the lads were lost to them fore'er." He paused, not sure if he should say any more, but then decided it would be best, however risky. "Mister Skinner told me, in confidence, mind ye, that he had nae faith that ye would e'er bring his lads back to him." Seeing the anger rise on Barlow's face, McTavish hastily added, "I dinna say that, Mister Barlow. 'Twas Mister Skinner. I'm only relatin' what he said. He told me he thought that ye'd forget aboot those two lads and just go off looking for your own child."

Barlow nodded. He could understand that much. Still, he thought it strange that they would not want to wait for a while before heading out, just in case he or someone else brought the children back in. "Well, then, Mister McTavish," he said, "I reckon you best send a rider out to bring them folks back."

"I canna do that, Mister Barlow," McTavish said with mock regret. "I canna misuse company employees in such a way. Having known Doctor McLoughlin, you should understand that."

"No, I can't understand that. You don't need to send an army out there, just one or two men. You got that many hangers-on here. No-accounts what ain't got nothin' better to do with their time."

"I canna spare any men, Mister Barlow. 'Tis that simple." He paused. "Besides, 'twould be foolish to bring them back here. If they are to get to the Oregon country before winter catches them on the trail somewhere, they canna afford the time to come back here. 'Twould be suicidal, as you should well know."

Barlow nodded. That, at least, made some sense. "So send a couple of men out with the youngn's here and get 'em back to their folks out there."

"Nae, Mister Barlow," he said tiredly. "I canna spare the men for that. And we dunna know where those people are."

"Hell, there ain't but one real trail 'tween here and

the Willamette Valley. It ain't marked real well, but it could be followed."

"And how would these men of mine, even if I could spare them, take care of the littlest youngster there. He's still on the teat, Mister Barlow."

"Coyote Woman here can go with 'em, nursin' the boy, jist like she's been doin'."

"You would trust some of my employees around this woman?" McTavish asked chidingly.

"She don't mean a damn thing to me, McTavish. Only reason I brung her along this far was to nurse the boy. It was her people who took them two young'ns, and it was her who was gonna raise at least one of 'em up to be a savage. I ain't aimin' to harm her none, but it wouldn't put me out none was somethin' to happen to her. I jist want to get these boys back to their folks where they belong. Surely even a man of your limited compassion can see that."

McTavish smarted under the insult, but he kept his feelings to himself. "I agree, they should be back with their families. Aye. But I canna do it." He paused, thinking. "Ye have my permission, however, to talk to any non-company employees who are hereabout and see if any of them can be talked into your scheme."

"You know goddamn well ain't a one of 'em gonna help me out. Not without your say-so, especially when I can't afford to pay 'em anything."

McTavish shrugged. " 'Tis the best I can offer ye, Mister Barlow. Now, if you dunna mind, I have many things to do."

Barlow stood there for some moments, letting his anger cool to a simmer. He felt like smashing McTavish to pieces. Then he decided that while the chances were almost nonexistent that he would be able to find anyone to take the boys to their families, he had to give it a try. If, as he was certain, it didn't work out, he would have another talk with Finan McTavish.

"Jist one more thing, McTavish," he finally said. "I

want quarters in the fort for me, the woman and the boys."

"It canna be done, Mr. Barlow. I . . ."

"You are walkin' the edge of a deep canyon here, McTavish," Barlow warned. "One little push and you'll go over the edge. These boys've been through enough already. They can use a real roof over their heads for a few nights. And the woman has to stay with them for reasons even you can figure out. Jist give us one of them small storerooms you got. We ain't gonna be here more'n a couple, three days."

McTavish nodded. If it would get Barlow out of his hair, he was willing to do this much. "See Mister Buxton. Tell him I said you were to have storeroom number two."

"Obliged." Barlow slapped his hat on and herded his little brood out. As he reached the office door, he turned and said, "You have a wee problem with your front door, Mister McTavish." He grinned as McTavish grimaced.

Ian Buxton was not, of course, very happy about having to help Barlow, even if it was such a small matter. However, he had changed his clothing since Barlow had knocked him down, and had no desire to get pummeled again, so he did what Barlow requested.

As he had known he would be, Barlow was unsuccessful in trying to recruit a couple of men to take Georgie and Sam Junior to the wagon. Several men had expressed some willingness—until they found out that Barlow had no money to pay for the mission. Then they quickly lost interest.

After two days, Barlow knew he would not find anyone to take on the task, so he paid McTavish another visit. The outside door to the office was repaired, though the workmanship was poor. In his anger and gloominess, Barlow considered tearing the door off again, but he realized that would do nothing to further his cause with McTavish, nor would it really make him feel any better.

"Nae luck on your quest, Mister Barlow?" McTavish asked as Barlow stalked into his office.

"Nope. You and I both knew that would happen. Now, I'm here to ask you agin to have some compassion for these two unfortunate young'ns and see that they get back to their families."

"As I've told you, Mr. Barlow, I canna do that. I have the company to think aboot, and with autumn almost here, I have to prepare my men for the winter trapping season."

"Don't you have some furs and such to ship back to Fort Vancouver?"

"Aye, but nae now. Ye should know we have little to be shipped there at this time of year. In the spring, that is a different story."

Barlow digested that, and nodded. It had been worth a try, he figured. "I reckon me and you got off on the wrong foot when I first come here, Mister McTavish. I admit, I might be a mite less than considerate and friendly from time to time. Not that I give a good goddamn about any of that. But I don't think it's fair of you to hold your dislikin' for me against them two boys."

McTavish cursed silently. He had, indeed, been holding his dislike for Barlow over the children, and he hated to be found out about it. Still, he was not about to change his mind just yet. The children were not his concern, and he was not about to help Barlow in any way. "Such insinuations offend me, Mister Barlow," he said stiffly.

"And such faint-hearted, parsimonious bastards like you offend me, McTavish."

"I am sorry, Mister Barlow," he said with a decided lack of sincerity. "But I must think of the company first. I canna do anything to help ye." He pursed his lips. "I dunna like to say this, but I feel I must. Ye found the children, Mister Barlow, and ye are the one who knows their kin, so 'tis your concern. 'Tis nae mine. And I would be grateful if ye were nae to come bursting in here anymore. Or I shall have you ejected by some of my men."

"I don't take kindly to threats, McTavish. Even a horse's ass like you should know that."

"That 'tis nae my concern either."

"It will be of your immediate concern, ol' hoss, if you do it agin. Take my meanin'?"

Fright appeared in McTavish's eyes, but he quickly blinked it away. "Aye. No go."

"We ain't done jawin' yet," Barlow said. He had given up on ever getting McTavish to do what he had asked here. He felt like pounding the smug factor into the ground, but that would not accomplish much, nor would it be likely to change McTavish's mind. It took a few moments for Barlow to resign himself to the fact that he would have to once more postpone his search for Anna for a spell so he could take the two young boys to their parents. He could not leave them here, and if McTavish would not have one of the fort workers do it, he had no other choice. However, there was a little problem in that.

"We're nae done?" McTavish asked peevishly.

"Nope." He paused, hating to ask. "Since you're not gonna be of any help to the boys, I reckon I'll have to take 'em myself." He disliked even more the sudden look of victory in McTavish's eyes. "But I be a mite short on supplies. I'll need some from you. Now I don't . . ."

"Dunna talk to me, lad. Talk to the trader. He'll be glad to sell ye whatever ye need."

"I got no specie, and you damn well know it, McTavish," Barlow snapped.

"Do tell," McTavish said with a condescending grin. "Well, then I'm afraid I canna help ye with this either. Good day."

"I don't need much, McTavish," Barlow said, seething.

"Wi'out money, ye'll nae get anything at all. I canna go around handing out goods to e'ery wanderer who comes through here. The company would have my head."

"Them boys'll die without some supplies."

"Perhaps ye can find work here that will bring in some cash. Then ye can buy whate'er ye will."

Sad and furious, Barlow turned for the door. Then he stopped and turned back. He had had just about enough of Finan McTavish.

18

IAN BUXTON WAS standing on the grounds outside the office, checking figures on his tote sheet when he heard a crash just behind him. The next thing he knew, he was on the ground, with something heavy laying on him. He quickly realized that it was his boss, Finan McTavish. "What in the bloody hell . . . ?" he mumbled as he tried to get out from under the seeming dead weight of the factor's body.

McTavish himself got up slowly, allowing his clerk to rise also. He stood for a moment, brushing dirt and glass off his clothes, before he realized that his head was bleeding. He pulled out a handkerchief and dabbed at the blood. Still dazed, he looked at the window of his office.

Barlow stood there, grinning. "Most folks I know, even crude fellers like me, use the door when they leave a room, McTavish," he said arrogantly. Then he vanished, only to reappear next to McTavish outside, having come out of the building the proper way. "Now, McTavish, about those supplies . . . ?"

"Mister Buxton," McTavish said, voice ragged, "please see that Mister Barlow gets the supplies he requires, but nae more than two hundred American dollars' worth." He looked warily, nervously at Barlow. "I trust ye will remove yourself from these premises as soon as ye have them. If ye do nae do so, I will have ye escorted out by armed men."

"No need for that, McTavish," Barlow said easily. "I got no hankerin' to linger here." He grinned. "Mister Buxton, at your leave, sir, we'll get started."

In less than an hour, Barlow was riding out of Fort Hall, right behind Coyote Woman, who carried Sam Junior, and Georgie. Behind Barlow were two new pack mules, loaded well, though not exorbitantly, with supplies. Barlow was dressed in a fine new cloth shirt, fringed buckskin pants, buffalo-hide moccasins and a new broad-brimmed hat. Buffalo bounded along, darting in and out of the mules, happy to be out of the confines of the white-walled adobe fort.

McTavish, now with a bandaged head, and Buxton watched the little procession as it left. When Barlow and the others were outside, McTavish breathed a sigh of relief.

The group headed west along the Snake River, skirting Old Man Verhoeven's tipi brothel. Barlow almost smiled.

He had felt the need for a woman last night, and had ridden over to Verhoeven's well after dark. He tied Beelzebub to a tree near Beatrix's sun-decorated lodge, and left Buffalo there. He stopped outside the tipi's flap. He was relieved when he heard her voice from inside. He had worried that she might not be here any longer. Based on what he could hear, too, Beatrix apparently was entertaining. Barlow didn't care. He pushed through the flap into the dim lodge, which was lit a little from a candle lantern sitting on a small wooden stool.

Beatrix was, indeed, with someone—a fat, smelly man who was kneeling between Beatrix's legs, stroking himself, trying to harden himself enough to enter her. He was having trouble, it seemed, and Beatrix seemed too bored to want to help him much. Barlow stepped up and grabbed the man by the back of his soiled shirt and hauled him up. The man's pants slid to his shoes, exposing his pitiful excuse for a love lance.

Beatrix's eyes widened in fear and surprise, but quickly those feelings left her, replaced by a great smile when she saw Barlow, who grinned back and winked.

Barlow hauled the other man along toward the entrance, the man shuffling with his pants down around his ankles. They stopped at the flap. "Pull your drawers up, ol' hoss. And go on home."

"But . . . I paid for . . ."

"You come on back tomorrow afternoon. Beatrix will be happy to fulfill your needs, boy."

"You ought to wait your goddamn turn, Mister," the man said, bending and struggling to pull his trousers up over his bulging belly.

"Well, I might've been willin' to do that had you shown any sign of actually gittin' somewhere with that little pecker of yours. Now go on, skedaddle, and maybe go practice gittin' it up."

"You son of a . . ."

Without moving his feet, Barlow pounded the man in the side of the head with his left hand, all the power coming straight from his back and shoulders.

The man sailed outside the lodge and landed in a heap on the ground.

"I said git, boy. And if you come back, I'll carve your gizzard out and feed it to my dog."

The man got up, saying, "You ain't got no . . ." He stopped and looked to his right in horror when Buffalo growled deeply. "Right," the man said. "I think I'll just mosey on back to the fort now." He eased away, keeping a decidedly wary eye on Barlow as he did.

"Good boy, Buffler," Barlow said with a smile. He closed the tipi flap, turned and walked over to where Beatrix yet lay, though she had now propped herself up on an elbow. She was still smiling at him. "Care for a bit of company, gal?" Barlow asked as he kicked off his moccasins.

"I'd like it." She paused. "I thought you never come back."

Barlow shucked off his shirt. "I only been by here once since I was with you that one time. Never had a chance."

"I'm glad you here now."

"So'm I." Barlow dropped his pants and stretched out over Beatrix, knees on either side of her hips, holding his torso up with his arms placed on each side of her head. He bent down and kissed her. She responded willingly, hungrily.

"I ain't of a mind to wait," Barlow gasped when he finished kissing her.

"Good. Now is good." Beatrix simply wanted to be filled by this man, who plugged her femaleness so well. "I help." She reached down and gently clasped his hard shaft, and guided it to the opening of her womanhood.

With a powerful plunge, Barlow sank himself to the full in her. Then he stopped, resting there a moment, relishing the sensations that rippled up his lance and warmed his entire body.

"Yes," Beatrix breathed, savoring the feel of his bigness filling her.

"You like that, eh?" Barlow asked, trying to sound smug, but revealing his lust instead.

"Much!"

"I must say that I like it a mighty powerful lot, too," Barlow breathed as he pulled back from her and began a rhythm of strong in and out movements.

Beatrix locked her ankles around the backs of his legs, just above the knees, and then rotated her hips in a well-timed counterpoint to his in-and-out thrusting.

It was not long before Barlow was roaring his delight as his climax approached, quickened, and then exploded in a bolt of lightning that shot through him and straight into Beatrix, who quivered with a small climax of her own.

As Barlow stretched out beside Beatrix, he said, "I hope I didn't disappoint you, ma'am."

"No, sir." She was still a little breathless. "Was good."

"Yes, Beatrix, it was that."

"Besides, there will be more." She grinned. "Soon."

Barlow laughed. "I think maybe you're right about that."

And by the time two more hours has passed, her astuteness was proven—much to her great satisfaction. They slept then, comfortable with each other.

Barlow was up before the dawn, and tried to get dressed without waking Beatrix, but she heard him rustling around.

She awoke, and smiled up at him. "Do you have to leave already?" she asked.

"Reckon so," he said, his annoyance at what life had dealt him lately returning.

"You don't have any time to spare?" Beatrix asked coyly, tossing aside the blanket, revealing her voluptuous body. She spread her legs a little, as an added enticement.

Barlow gulped. There was no love between him and Beatrix, and both knew that. But she was a fine woman in the robes, and he saw no reason whatsoever that they could not enjoy each other's company, despite what she was and his mission. Then he grinned, too. "Reckon I can spare a few minutes."

He rejoined her on the bed of robes and blankets, and they soon coupled again, their passions rising to a blistering, shuddering crescendo that had both uttering animal-like sounds.

Soon after, however, he was dressed and riding back to the fort. Light had not yet broken. The problems he faced trickled back into his mind, already blunting the enjoyment he had had with Beatrix. He knew by now that he would certainly not find anyone to take the two boys to their parents, and that he would have to do it. He did not look forward to that. It wasn't that he had anything against the youngsters. He just did not want to waste another couple of weeks or a month trying to find Judith Dockery and Cora Skinner. He wanted to get back to looking for Anna. But he couldn't just leave the boys here, so he knew he would have to take on this task. It didn't, however, mean he had to like it.

When he got back to their quarters at the fort, he explained to Coyote Woman what had to be done. "I ain't of a mind to try'n force you to come along with us," he said. "But I will if I have to. You know the littlest boy needs nursin'. So I'm askin' you to come along with me and take care of him like you've been doin'."

"Why should I do this?" Coyote Woman asked. "If I refuse, will you kill me?"

"Reckon that wouldn't do much good now, would it," Barlow responded. "But if you refuse, I expect I could tie you up and haul you along. That wouldn't be comfortable for neither of us."

"I will go," she said. It was evident in her voice and on her face that she knew she had no choice.

"Good. And I'd be obliged was you to give me no trouble along the way." He paused. "You seem to have taken a shine to Sam Junior. I'm wagerin' you'd not want to do anything to endanger that chil'."

Coyote Woman nodded. She could say nothing else.

"And I promise you, woman," Barlow continued, "that if you help me and don't cause no ruckus along the way, I'll set you free as soon as we find them boys' folks. Once they're settled, I'll take you back down toward your people. Once we're within' spittin' distance of your village, I'll let you ride on—with that mule you've been usin'. And I'll go off my own way, lookin' for my Anna."

"That is good," Coyote Woman said, her voice gaining a little strength. She did not completely trust this white man, but he had never mistreated her, nor had he lied to her as best she could tell. She thought she could believe him now, though she was fatalistic enough to know that if he did not do what he had promised, she would be able to do little about it.

Barlow glanced back once after they had passed the prostitutes' lodges. He couldn't see Beatrix, and figured she was busy. He shook his head at the strangeness of how well he and the strumpet had hit it off.

Without a definite place to go to, Barlow did not push his charges very much. They did not dawdle, but they did not work the animals—or themselves—too hard. As Barlow had reminded McTavish, there was only one basic way for the Skinner-Dockery party to go. There was a trail of sorts, formed by the men who carried supplies and furs between Fort Vancouver and Fort Hall. It wasn't very discernable, but it could be followed. So, unless they wandered off the path somehow, Barlow figured it was just a matter of time before he caught up with them. Especially since their wagon was moving as slowly as it was. Though the wagon had more than two weeks' head start, Barlow and his small party—even without pushing it—could move twice as fast on a regular basis.

Two days after they left the fort, Barlow began ranging out a little ahead of Coyote Woman and the two boys. He had planned to do it earlier, but wanted to make sure they were far enough from the post so that Coyote Woman would not get it into her mind to turn tail and run back there seeking help. Barlow thought she would stay true to her word—if for no other reason than to protect Sam Junior—but he did not fully trust her either.

Though he did not think he would find White Bear's band of Shoshonis out here, he had to in good conscience, keep looking. So he would rove in a large arc from the Snake River out into the open, searching, always searching. Buffalo traveled with him, not content to plod along with Coyote Woman and the boys.

Besides watching for Shoshoni villages, Barlow used his excursions to hunt, so they always had fresh meat, and to keep an eye out each afternoon for a suitable place to spend the night.

After two and a half weeks on the trail, Barlow was beginning to despair that he would ever find the wagon. He had not considered that possibility earlier, so he had given no thought as to what he would do if that occurred. Now he began to wonder, and the options were not good. If he decided he could not find the wagon, he had two basic choices—turn back and try to find someone at Fort Hall to care for the children; or press ahead and try to find someone to care for the children in the Willamette Valley. Somewhere along in his wanderings, he decided that if he had to make the choice, he would keep going. Doing so would take him farther away from Anna again, but there was always a chance that the emigrants he sought might find their way there. Even if they didn't, Barlow knew of many people with whom he could entrust the children.

So it was with great relief that just under three weeks from the fort, he spotted the lone wagon lumbering along slowly ahead of him. He didn't need his spyglass to check. There could be no other ox-drawn wagons out here; no other wagons of any kind. He turned and kicked Beelzebub into a trot, as Buffalo raced alongside. When they reached Coyote Woman and the boys, Barlow hurriedly explained what he had seen. Georgie's eyes widened with hope and joy, and even Coyote Woman looked interested.

"So let's move," he said, leading the way off. They did not trot or gallop, but they did walk a lot faster than they had up to now on this trip. Within an hour, they were within hailing distance of the wagon, and Barlow rode out a few yards ahead of the others, calling, "Hello, the wagon!"

19

BRINGING UP THE rear, Hope Skinner was the first to hear Barlow calling. She turned at the sound, wondering—and worrying a little. Who would be calling to them way out here? she wondered. Then she thought she recognized Barlow, though at first she couldn't be sure.

Barlow hollered again, and this time Hope was certain. She spun, "Stop! George, stop!"

Her son, up by the head of the ox team, stopped the animals and turned. His eyes widened when he looked at where his mother was pointing. He hurried back to stand next to Hope. "Who is it?" he asked.

"Mister Barlow! And he's not alone!"

The others had come into view now, behind Barlow. "Lord Almighty!" Hope breathed, her heart thumping, "That's little Georgie!"

"By God, Gran, you're right!" Judith said, moving up to stand next to Hope, on the opposite side from her father.

"But who's that other one with him?" George asked, shading his eyes to see better. "It looks like an Injun woman. That reprobate!"

"Don't be so judgmental, son," Hope chided him

mildly. "There may be a perfectly good reason she's along. Other than the one your profane mind has conjured up."

Georgie had seen the wagon and with a nod from Barlow, had slapped the mule into a trot, eager to get to his mother. He tumbled off the mule into her arms, before the animal had fully stopped. Georgie's father had to grab the reins to keep the mule from running off.

Mother and son hugged and cried, while Hope, George and the other children gathered happily around. Judith, however, stood staring out toward Barlow, anxiously looking for her son. She could not see him, though, just Barlow and the Indian woman. She turned away, head down, moving away from the others.

Barlow loped up and pulled Beelzebub to a stop next to her. "Miss Judith," he said quietly. When she raised her tear-stained face toward him, he said, "Don't you want to see that young'n of yours?"

"What?" Judith asked, confused. "What do you . . . ?"

Barlow nodded toward Coyote Woman. "Sam Junior's with her. He's on her . . ."

But Judith was no longer listening. She had whirled and was running toward Coyote Woman.

The Paiute, realizing that Judith must be Sam Junior's mother, stopped the mule and started climbing off the animal when she saw Judith heading toward her. She was afraid that Judith would pull her off the mule in the haste to get to her child.

But Judith stopped, bouncing excitedly, trying to figure out how to get Sam Junior's cradleboard off the woman's back, or get the boy out of it.

Coyote Woman quickly slid the cradleboard off her shoulders, and handed it to Judith. The white woman hugged Sam Junior—and the cradleboard—all at once, whispering endearments to her son. She hurried off to join the others, as everyone expressed their joy at the return of both boys.

Still mounted, Barlow stood back out of the way, not wanting to intrude on the joyous reunion. He half wanted to just ride out and head back to Fort Hall, but the other part of him had enough reason to know that it was getting close to dark and it would make sense for him to spend the night with the Skinners and Dockerys. Plus he hoped that he would get a decent meal out of it all. He was tired of eating nothing but roasted meat.

The celebrating went on for a quite a while. In the midst of it, Judith managed to get Sam Junior out of the cradleboard, and was hugging him half to death, as far as Barlow could tell. Georgie looked as if he was about to be smothered in his mother's embrace.

For Barlow, this was a tremendously bittersweet moment. He was, of course, very glad that the families had had this reunion, and could well understand their somewhat lengthy celebration. He was even quite pleased that he had been the one to bring this happy reunion about. But the celebrating, and the reason why, continually reminded him that, so far, he had failed in bringing about the reunion he most wanted—that with his daughter, Anna. He could not help but think how happy he would have been if he had been able to find her and bring her out of some Indian village instead of these two boys. Or better, in addition to them.

After some time, the welcoming wound down. George Skinner walked over and stuck out his hand. "I'm much obliged to you for bringin' my son and grandson back, Mister Barlow."

Barlow shrugged, a little embarrassed.

"I expect you'll be ridin' on now with your squaw, then?" Skinner asked, voice shifting from genuine thanks to disgust.

Barlow looked around, chewing on his lower lip as he battled his anger. It was dusk off to the east, and it would be catching up to them soon. Finally he looked back at Skinner. "Do you always make damnfool assumptions, ol' hoss? Or is this some kind of new skill you're tryin' to develop?"

"What the hell's that supposed to mean?"

"It means, you dim-witted piece of shit, that if it

wasn't for that woman over there, Sam Junior wouldn't be in his mama's arms right now."

"What the hell's that Injin woman got to do with anything?" Skinner demanded. He hated to be made a fool of, though Barlow seemed to have an easy job of it.

"What she has to do with it, son," Hope said, walking up from behind to stand next to Skinner, "is that Sam Junior is still on the teat, which you'd know if you paid any attention to such things. And that Injin woman was nursin' him. Without that, your grandson would've gone under a while back."

"And you ain't sportin' with her?" Skinner asked, not taking his eyes off Barlow.

"Whether I am or whether I ain't is no concern of yours, ol' hoss," Barlow said flatly. "And you'd do well to keep your silence when it concerns other folks doin's. Ain't too many folks I know appreciate busybodies."

Before Skinner could say anything else, Hope asked, "What're your plans, Mister Barlow?"

"Well, Miss Hope, I expect I'll stay out here the night, which is comin' up on us pretty quickly. In the mornin', I reckon I'll head on back down the trail. I still got to find Anna, you now."

"Well, you stay with us tonight. The least we can do for you is see you get a good meal."

"I'd be obliged for that. I've had a hankerin' for your cookin'." Barlow grinned a little.

"Then we're powerfully pleased to have you." She half turned. "George, we'll stay the night right up the trail there," she pointed, "in that clump of trees."

"But, Ma . . ."

"Unless you have somethin' sensible to say, just shut your trap and start movin' the wagon."

Skinner slunk away, insulted and embarrassed, the feelings exacerbated by Barlow's condescending grin at him.

Within half an hour, the camp was set up. A big fire was going, and the three white women were preparing a meal. Before the cooking started, Coyote Woman went to Judith, who was trying to work, as well as keep an eye on two-and-a-half-year-old Elizabeth, and an extra watch over Sam Junior. The Paiute said, "I watch boy for you. I watch good."

Judith's eyes reflected her horror, and she grabbed Sam Junior up in her arms, holding him protectively.

From where he was tending the mules, Barlow had overheard. Seeing Judith's fear, he walked over to her and said, "It'll be all right, Miss Judith."

"But she's . . ."

"She could have harmed Sam Junior many a time between the time we left her village and today. She didn't. And she won't do so now. She'll take good care of him."

Tentatively, fearfully, Judith held the boy out. Coyote Woman took Sam Junior and cooed to him. She looked almost happy as she moved off, jiggling the boy in her hands and singing some tune in her own language.

"You sure it'll be all right, Mr. Barlow?" Judith asked.

Barlow nodded and went back to his work. Buffalo took a position about halfway between Coyote Woman and Barlow, and lay down with a soft grunt.

Soon everyone was sitting on the ground around the fire. Skinner was not pleased that Coyote Woman was allowed in on the mostly family gathering, but Judith had insisted, and Hope had backed her up. Barlow watched that little exchange with interest, as he saw the young woman and her grandmother traded what seemed to be significant glances with each other. Those looks reinforced Barlow's earlier suspicions—that the two women knew about each other, and him. They did not seem upset with each other, or him, which he thought was a good thing. But it still surprised him.

"So," Barlow asked, as he spooned in some of the excellent, thick, deer-meat stew Hope had fixed up, "why'd you folks leave Fort Hall so soon?"

"Had no choice," Skinner said hotly. "Now, I recall you sayin' not too long ago that a man doesn't go pokin' into the affairs of others."

"I did say that. But I was referrin' to people snoopin' into business that don't concern them."

"This don't concern you."

"When I have to go traipsin' over half the western territories lookin' for you to bring your children back to you, ol' hoss, it sure as hell does concern me. If you had waited back at Fort Hall for another couple of weeks, you would have got your young'ns back a long time ago, and I could've been out lookin' for my Anna again by now."

"What my son says is true, at least in part, Mr. Barlow," Hope said quietly. "We was heartbroke over the loss of them yonkers. And, well, I'm powerfully ashamed to admit it, but I—and the rest of us—allowed ourselves to be convinced that we would never see the boys again. After more than a month in the clutches of those savag . . ." She glanced at Coyote Woman, who pretended to ignore it. "In the clutches of those Injins, we became certain that their fate was sealed."

Barlow nodded. He could understand that to some degree. Of course, was it he, he would have stayed at the fort or its vicinity as long as it took to have proof of some kind that finding the children would be hopeless. But these people were not him. They were new to this country and knew little about it except what they had heard in stories and tales, and the men at the fort would almost certainly play on their fears as a cruel practical joke.

"Stayin' at the fort was not an option, Mister Barlow," Hope continued. "That devilish Mister McTavish made that clear to us. We know that winter's comin' on pretty fast, and from what we could learn, we would be hard pressed to make the Oregon country before being caught up in winter on the trail if we left when we did. It seemed we had little choice but to push ahead with our journey, mournin' the loss of our yonkers."

That made more sense to Barlow. He could picture McTavish wanting a couple of families of emigrants out of his vicinity so he would not have to be responsible for them. It was an unpleasant thought, but one he thought McTavish was quite capable of.

Barlow nodded. "It's true that winter'll be here before long. And if you don't press hard, you sure as hell will git caught out in the open by the snow and cold. I'll tell you somethin' else, too, folks, I don't think you're gonna git that wagon over the mountains northwest of here. Even the freight hauled between Fort Hall and Fort Vancouver goes by mule or horse."

The other white adults cast concerned glances around at each other, wondering for the thousandth time what they had gotten themselves into.

"Do you suggest we just abandon it, Mister Barlow?" Skinner asked. "All our possessions, all we own?" He made it sound as if it were almost ridiculous.

"I reckon it would be hard," Barlow said very quietly. "It ain't easy losin' everything dear to you." In a stronger voice he added, "But you have to look at it this way—is keepin' all those possessions worth the life of everyone here?"

"That's hogwash, Mister Barlow." Skinner snorted.

"Shut up, George," Hope snapped. "Thinkin' back on it, I never heard Mister McTavish say any of those things. You simply told us that's what he said. And, since you had neglected to tell him about Georgie and Sam Junior at first, I'm beginnin' to believe you have no concerns for anyone other than yourself. You were the one who talked us into leavin' the safety of that fort—without the two boys, and without a guide of any kind. Your hardheadedness may very well have cost the lives of Sam Junior and Georgie. And perhaps the rest of us. You're as bad as your father, George. Unconcerned about anything except what benefits you. Between you and your father, we might all have perished on this trip. You are a thorough embarrassment of a son, and I am ashamed not only that I brung you into the world, but that I have listened to you so often on this cursed trip."

The other adults sat in stunned silence. Even Skinner was too shocked to speak.

"But no more, George," Hope said, catching a fresh wind. "No more. If Mister Barlow says we should abandon this wagon, it will stay right where it sits now, with all its contents."

"You'd trust that son of a . . ."

"Hush your mouth, son!" Hope said, enraged. "He has been nothing but a gentleman and a boon to us. You have brung nothing but trouble, even *causin'* half of it with your foolishness." She paused, and looked at Barlow. "I know this is a grand imposition, Mister Barlow," she said apologetically, "considerin' your quest and all. But I now realize that our chances of making the Oregon country are remote without your help. I implore you, sir, to take pity on a foolish old woman and lead us out of this wilderness to this Willamette Valley you have mentioned. Would you do that for us, Mister Barlow?"

Barlow wished she had not phrased it that way. It left him in a bind. All he wanted to do was to try to find Anna. But, again, he could not leave these people out here like this. These pilgrims would never be able to make the rest of the journey on their own.

"I promised Coyote Woman I'd take her back to her people as payment for havin' helped with Sam Junior," he said lamely. "I don't want to go back on my word."

"Give her a mule and some supplies and let her go back on her own," Judith suddenly interjected. "She's an Injin, and should be able to make her own way."

"Or," Hope tossed in, "if that is unsatisfactory, she is welcome to travel with us to the Oregon country. When we get there, you and she can decide what she will do."

Barlow thought that over, and saw no problem with either plan. He would rather not be saddled with Coyote Woman all the way to the Willamette Valley, but he would not force her out across these almost trackless lands on her own. He turned to her. "What do you say, Coyote Woman?" he asked. "You want to head back to your people on your own? Or travel with these fine folks to the Oregon country?"

"I go with them. If all right."

"You're welcome to come, Coyote Woman," Hope said.

"Good." For the first time since Barlow had taken her out of the Northern Paiute village, he saw Coyote Woman smile, really smile.

"So, Mister Barlow?" Hope asked. "Will you help us?" She paused, and then brazenly added, "The trip should be as pleasant as we can make it, I can assure you of that." She smiled, looked at her granddaughter and then back to the former mountain man.

Barlow glanced at Judith, who was smiling boldly back at him. Then he glanced at Hope, who was still smiling. *Yes*, he thought, *this likely would be a most pleasant trip.* He nodded. "I'll do it."

As they pulled out the next morning—Barlow having explained that there was no need to get rid of the wagon just yet—he waited until the others were on their way, and he stopped. Dismounting, he knelt next to Buffalo and gazed eastward—to where he figured Anna was—and stayed there for some minutes, silently telling Anna not to despair, that he would come for her just as soon as he could.

With some regret, he mounted Beelzebub and turned westward, saddened by the knowledge that he would have no chance to even look for Anna again until at least the next spring. It would be a bittersweet journey to the Willamette Valley.

J. R. ROBERTS
THE GUNSMITH

Explore the exciting Old West with one of the men who made it wild!

JAKE LOGAN
TODAY'S HOTTEST ACTION WESTERN!